DAUGHTERS OF THE MOON

AR BL 5.7

the becoming

Pts. 6.0

(12)

LYNNE EWING

HYPERION/NEW YORK

CPLYA

Also in the
DAUGHTERS OF THE MOON
series:

Volo® is a registered trademark of Disney Enterprises, Inc.
The Volo colophon is a trademark of Disney Enterprises, Inc.

First Edition
3 5 7 9 10 8 6 4 2
Printed in the United States of America

Reinforced binding

Library of Congress Cataloging-in-Publication Data
Ewing, Lynne.
The becoming / Lynne Ewing.—1st ed.
p.   cm. — (Daughters of the moon; 12)
Summary: Tianna no longer knows who to trust when good and evil forces fight over
her and rush her toward an uncertain, but crucial, destiny—toward either the moon
goddess, Selene, or the ancient evil known as the Atrox.
ISBN 0-7868-1892-1 (trade)
[1. Supernatural—Fiction. 2. Los Angeles (Calif.)—Fiction.] I. Title.
PZ7.E965Be 2004
[Fic]—dc22
2004041976

Visit www.volobooks.com

For Tina Jeffries

In the beginning of the ancient world Prometheus stole a glowing ember from the sacred fire of the gods and gave it to all mortals to protect them from the cold of night. But Zeus, the king of the gods, became angry that such a gift had been taken, and in vengeance he decided to balance the blessing of fire with a curse. He ordered Hephaestus to sculpt a woman of exquisite beauty whose destiny was to bring great sorrow upon the human race. She was to be named Pandora.

As Hephaestus molded the clay into a stunning female, a primordial evil called the Atrox watched covetously from the shadows. Once she was complete, Hermes took Pandora to Epimetheus, the brother of Prometheus, and offered her to him, as a present from Zeus. When he saw the beautiful Pandora, Epimetheus forgot his brother's warning not to accept any gifts from the great god, and took her for his bride.

For her dowry, the gods had given Pandora a huge, mysterious storage jar, but the Atrox knew what lay inside. At the wedding feast, it shrewdly aroused her curiosity and convinced her to open the lid. And when she did, countless evils flew into the world. Only hope remained inside, a consolation for all the evils that had been set free. But no one saw the demon sent by the Atrox to destroy hope and kidnap Pandora. Selene, the goddess of the Moon, however, finally heard Pandora's cries and stopped the demonic creature.

The Atrox studied this defeat and envisioned a way to inflict even greater suffering upon the world. It journeyed to the edge of night and found the three sister Fates, goddesses older than time, who spun the threads that predetermined the course of every life. Once they had agreed to the Atrox's plan, their decision became irrevocable. Even great Zeus could not alter their ruling. Only Selene dared to scorn their decree, and she alone vowed to change destiny.

CHAPTER ONE

T

IANNA PRESSED AGAINST the dusty door-jamb and studied the faces of the kids strolling up and down Melrose Avenue. She didn't want anyone she knew to see her leave the purple-painted storefront. She slipped her sunglasses on, swung her backpack over her shoulder, and quickly ducked behind four girls waiting at an espresso stand. The aroma of coffee mingled with the scent of sandalwood still clinging to her from the incense in the fortuneteller's shop. Now she wished she had never gone inside.

She glanced over her shoulder. Madame Oskar stood in the doorway staring after her, the beads on her turban catching the late afternoon light. Her lips moved, and her long fingers marked the air as if she were sending a curse. She must have glimpsed something terrifying in Tianna's future. Why else would she have thrown the crystal ball across the room?

Tianna had seen only churning mists inside the globe and had figured it was just a silly prop. But Madame Oskar had winced, her eyes wide in horror. She had yelled hysterically in a language Tianna didn't understand. Then, suddenly, she had grabbed the crystal ball and hurled it at the wall, toppling a line of tambourines on a shelf. The glass had exploded, scattering sharp fragments across the room, and the sun, refracted through the shards, had gilded the walls with prismatic lights that had seemed menacing despite their rainbow hues.

Now Tianna brushed at a nick on her cheek and wondered what had upset Madame. Normally she would never have paid a psychic to tell her future, because Serena could read tarot cards with surprising accuracy, but Tianna wasn't ready to share her problems with her friends yet.

Her life in Los Angeles had become too unsettled, and she was getting the urge to move on. In the past, when this uneasy feeling had taken hold, she had always trusted the mysterious voice inside her that told her to leave. This time she didn't understand why it should be urging her to go. She had friends, a boyfriend, and a good home—everything she had wanted since her own family had been brutally murdered.

She sighed heavily, feeling defeated. She had hoped Madame might help her understand her rising apprehension, but the session had only made the foreboding grow. Now she felt as if she couldn't run fast or far enough to escape the fate looming in her future.

She started to cross the street just as the light turned red. She stopped at the curb and breathed in the spicy aroma of chai tea from the Emporium. To top off her troubles, Derek had asked her late that afternoon if she thought they were ready to have sex. Sex? Yikes! Where had he gotten such an idea? Had she done something to make him think that was what she wanted? She cared for him, but she didn't feel their relationship had reached that level yet. Had it?

Her thoughts were broken by the sudden sense that someone was staring at her. She pushed her sunglasses to the top of her head, turned, and squinted into the setting sun. She had expected to see Madame still glaring at her, but a metal gate now covered the entrance to her shop, and a large sign in the window read *Closed*.

The feeling of being watched grew stronger. Tianna surveyed the faces of the kids crowding the sidewalk behind her. No one was looking at her. Still, she couldn't shrug the curious sensation.

She lifted the silver amulet hanging around her neck to see if it was warning her of danger. She studied the moon etched in the metal, and the memory of the night that Maggie Craven had given her the charm came back to her, filling her with sad comfort.

"Tu es dea, filia lunae," Maggie had told her in Latin. Tianna had been stunned when Maggie had translated the words. "You are a Goddess, a Daughter of the Moon."

But, now more than ever, Tianna was certain it had been a mistake. She felt like a fraud—just a girl, not a goddess. Besides, she was the outsider; she hadn't been born a Daughter, like Serena, Vanessa, Jimena, and Catty. Selene, the goddess of the moon, had looked down and decided to make her a Daughter because she had saved the others from the Followers of an ancient evil called the Atrox.

Tianna sighed, her chest hollow; she wished she could see Maggie now. The woman had been more than her mentor and guide. She had given Tianna a sense of belonging. Before Maggie disappeared, she had been showing the others how to use their gifts. Selene had given each of them a power to help them fight the Atrox. Serena read thoughts, Vanessa became invisible, Jimena had premonitions, and Catty traveled through time. Tianna also had a power. She had the ability to move things, but her telekinetic power hadn't been a gift from Selene, so where had it come from? Was she just a freak of nature?

She clasped the amulet, and the metal purred

against her palm. The charm glowed and pulsed in warning when Followers were near, but it wasn't alerting her to danger now; it sensed her blue mood and was trying to comfort her. How pathetic was that? Other kids had dogs, cats, brothers, sisters, and friends to console them. She had a stone.

The light turned green, and she started across the street, hating the way she was indulging in so much self-pity; but her low spirits had become inescapable.

On the next corner three bare-chested guys leaned against a red convertible, their skin pink with sunburn. They were obviously checking her out.

She had become accustomed to bold stares. People frequently gawked at her, startled by her beauty, and these guys were totally looking her up and down. She was wearing black cowboy boots, low-slung cargo shorts, and a skimpy top. She had not dressed that way to pick up guys, though. The January day was sweltering, with record-high temperatures, in the nineties, hot even for L.A.

She brushed her hands through her hair, trying to catch a breeze, and her waistband slipped down, exposing her flat, tanned stomach.

The largest of the three guys mistook her gesture for a come-on. He jumped off the hood of the car and started after her, his steps sure and cocky, his flip-flops snapping against his heels. He placed an unwanted hand on her bare waist, his grimy palm damp with sweat.

"Hey, I've seen you around. I'm Doug."

She twisted away. "Go bother someone who likes losers."

His friends whooped and laughed. "Forget her, Doug!"

"I'm just trying to be friendly." Doug grinned, showing off perfect capped teeth. He was wearing too much aftershave.

"I'm not in the mood to be sociable." Tianna tried to ease away from him, but he kept up with her, his fingers tickling her elbow, body pressing against her back.

"I've watched you at Planet Bang. You're a great dancer. Do you want to go out?" The simple question felt too suggestive, as if he had other things in mind.

"Get lost." Tianna quickened her stride.

But her brush-off seemed only to embolden him. She could feel him shoving through the crowd after her like a column of heat.

Suddenly, hands grabbed her shoulders, the grip unbearably strong, and forced her into a narrow passage between two dress shops. Instinctively she swung, trying to defend herself. She kicked and toppled a green trash can, spilling bottles, cans, and wrappers. She started to trip, but whoever held her kept her balanced.

She pitched back and forth, punching and trying to wrench free. The hands holding her threw her against the brick wall and released her. She whipped around, slugging air, then stopped.

There was no one there.

She blinked. Doug was back with his friends at the convertible, staring at her, dumbfounded. "Dang, you're freaky."

If he hadn't attacked her, then who had? She bit her lip and curled her fingers into fists, holding back her power. Energy raged inside her, straining for release, and finally settled back. She drew a long breath, grateful she hadn't created the scene her mind had pictured: Doug flat on his back with pedestrians stepping around him.

At last she picked up her backpack and started toward the sidewalk, her legs shaky.

Two girls in motorcycle boots and hotpants eased away from her. The chocolate ice cream in their cones was melting over their fingers. They stared at her, uncertain.

Tianna smiled, trying to reassure them, but after the way she had been shadowboxing and fighting off an invisible attacker, they probably thought she'd been smoking PCP and was a danger, lost in some drug-induced psychosis.

She hurried around them, aware of their uneasy eyes, but she had worries of her own to consider. The mysterious hands baffled her. What had caused the strange sensation? Stress affected Vanessa's ability to control her gift. Now Tianna wondered if the same thing could be happening to her. She used telekinesis to move objects, but did that mean her mind formed invisible hands to do the work? Her skills had been out of control since she'd broken her collarbone. The fracture had healed, but her powers were still giving her problems. Had she attacked herself? She shuddered, wondering why she would.

She darted into a side street, anxious to be home, then turned down an alley, taking a shortcut. The security lights hadn't come on yet, and shadows cradled the walls and stoops. She stepped around puddles and trash bins, a feeling of dark apprehension growing inside her.

Near the back of a seafood restaurant, the sweet-sour smell of garbage filled the air, and a strange tension curled around her. She took three more steps, and her uneasiness turned to alarm. Something was wrong. She started to shiver, but not from cold. The breeze was still warm with heat from the day. It was as if her body had sensed some danger that her mind had not yet perceived. Her nerves thrummed as she studied the shadows that lay in front of her.

A soft whisper, no more than a breeze

against her ear, made her glance over her shoulder. A phantom piece of darkness slipped toward her. She froze, her heart racing. Not even a rat could do that, but a powerful Follower could.

Some Followers were shape-shifters who could dissolve into shadow and blend with the night. Maybe one was trailing her now, taking its time to tease her and relish her fear, because it knew she was alone and vulnerable.

The inky figure twisted closer, sliding over brick walls and window sills. She watched, drawn to it. Her amulet glowed, the vibration jarring her from her stupor. The shadow had come too close. If she reached out now, she could touch its velvet blackness.

She flinched and stepped back, then spun around and sprinted away, concentrating on the red and pink neon lights pulsing at the other end of the alley. Her boots felt like lead weights clomping on the asphalt.

The air shifted next to her and she had the odd sensation of someone racing alongside her. Sprays of muddy water wet her legs, as if another runner had splashed through the puddles beside her. Phantom footsteps thrashed over bundled newspapers, scattering loose pages, but she didn't pause to see what ran with her.

She could stop and use her power to defend herself, but what would happen in the instant it took to build up energy? Instead, she put her faith in her ability to run. She picked up speed, breathing through her mouth, and kept her eyes riveted on the street at the end of the alley.

Then, without warning, darkness unfurled around her, blocking sight and sound; still, she didn't pause. She never broke her stride. She vaulted forward, her muscles tight and burning with the effort. Her foot landed wrong, and she twisted her ankle. Intense pain shot up her leg, but she kept loping forward, skipping and hopping.

At last she broke into the light. Traffic sounds crashed around her, and garish neon signs throbbed. She blinked, adjusting her eyes to the brightness, and almost collided with three middle-aged women holding shopping bags and waiting to board a bus.

"Sorry," she said and turned, ignoring their scowls. She stared back down the alley, a cold sweat prickling her forehead.

One by one, security lights came on, but she saw nothing unusual, not even an odd blur of shadow. Stray cats pawed at garbage, their tails flicking the air, and a busboy emptied trash into the Dumpster.

Tianna stood there, spent and trembling. What was going on?

CHAPTER TWO

THE BRIGHT BEAM FROM car headlights washed across the large Tudor house, then swept away, leaving the tall, narrow windows dark and menacing again. Tianna hurried up the brick path to the porch, the sweet scents of jasmine and honeysuckle breezing around her. She fumbled through her backpack and pulled out her keys. She lived there with two other foster kids, Shannon and Todd.

The phone started ringing inside. She unlocked the door and hurried in, then crossed the tiled entry to the gloomy living room and grabbed the receiver.

"Hello," she said. A dial tone answered her, and she dropped the receiver back into its cradle, wondering who had been calling.

Silence and shadows gathered around her. She had always been bold and unafraid, but suddenly, being alone in the huge house made her uneasy. Using only a thought, she switched on a Tiffany lamp behind the couch, grateful her telekinetic skills were working normally again. Unfortunately, the dull orange glow did little to light the cheerless room. The air felt stuffy, still filled with the depressing smells of disinfectant, medicine, and illness, all sad reminders of Todd's last night at home before he was rushed to the hospital.

She hurried to the kitchen to escape the odor. Her power pushed ahead of her, switching on overhead lights and opening the swinging door. Her foster mother, Mary, knew about her strange ability to move things and had asked her not to use it, but when Mary wasn't around, Tianna treated her gift like any modern convenience.

A note sat propped on the counter in front of a red bowl and a tall glass, reminding Tianna to take her vitamins and her energy drink. Tianna picked up the bowl and tossed the capsules and tablets in the sink. She didn't understand Mary's insistence that she gulp down so many pills and drink such stinky herbal concoctions. It was starting to annoy her. Worse, she could no longer bear the pity in Mary's eyes. She might have been an orphan, but she didn't need to be reminded of it by Mary's consoling looks.

Tianna rubbed her hands over her face in frustration. Why was she so upset with Mary? She was only trying to help her. This was Tianna's chance to live a normal life, and she was letting everything unravel again. What was wrong with her?

She picked up the glass, determined to drink the green sludge, but when she tore off the plastic cover, the foul odor made her wince. The liquid smelled like the bottom of a goldfish bowl that hadn't been cleaned for months. She dumped it in the sink, then willed the water on. A steady stream flowed, and she started the garbage disposal.

As the motor whirred, uninvited memories of the night Todd had been taken to the hospital seeped into her mind. She clutched the edge of the sink and tried to ignore the memory of him on the gurney, a blood-pressure cuff around his bone-thin arm, his small face lost under the clear plastic mask that fed him oxygen. Todd had stared at her, his eyes unfocused, his lips moving, trying to tell her something. What had he been saying? She worried that he had been accusing her of hurting him.

She had been playing Monopoly with him when he had collapsed suddenly. How could he have become so ill so quickly? She swallowed hard, trying to escape the nagging guilt that her haywire power had done something to him. She had gone to the hospital twice to visit him and find out, but both times he had been sleeping.

Her anxiety grew, and she headed back through the living room, turning off the lights, garbage disposal, and water with her mind. Near the base of the stairs, her cell phone began to ring from her bedroom upstairs. She bounded up the steps, not sure where she had left it this time, and burst into her room just as it stopped. Before she could pick it up to see who had called, the house phone began ringing again. She started back downstairs, but paused in the hallway.

A phone rang in Mary's bedroom. Did she dare go inside to answer it? She'd never been in Mary's room before. That seemed odd, now that she thought about it. She supposed Mary was a very private person. The ringing stopped, but her urge to snoop around didn't leave her. The few times she had seen Mary enter or leave the room, Mary had been secretive, as if she were sneaking in and out. The door was always closed. What was in there that Mary didn't want her to see?

She knew she should respect Mary's privacy, and besides, she didn't have time to look around—she had to get ready to go out with Derek—but her fingers curled around the doorknob anyway. It turned easily in her hand, and she slipped inside.

The air was cold and dank, and filled with a

strong, musky odor. She wondered if Mary kept a humidifier running all day. Tianna flicked on the wall switch, and dim light crept over a soiled carpet.

She drew back, startled. The walls were blank, stark gray, and stained. A worn pink blanket spotted with coffee spills covered a small bed. Shoeboxes lined the room, and numerous shopping bags from pricey stores crowded a corner, filled with clothes, the tags still attached. Slacks, sweaters, and dresses were crammed into the closet, and suits rolled into bundles lay stacked across the floor, giving the impression that Mary wore an outfit only once, then stuffed it away and took something new from one of the shopping bags.

The top of her dresser was a mess of receipts, bills, and medical journals, and was further cluttered with a line of toppled white Styrofoam heads, each with a wig tacked on. Tianna hadn't known until now that Mary's hair wasn't her own.

Unfinished paint-by-numbers kits lay

scattered across the floor. Specks of red and dried paintbrushes dotted the carpet. Tianna wondered briefly if Mary aspired to being an artist.

But Tianna was surprised most by what was missing. Maggie had told her that Mary had lost her family, yet there wasn't a single photo or memento on the wall or dresser.

The phone rang again, and she jumped. Only then did she realize how nervous she had become from her trespassing. She didn't answer. Instead she turned off the light and eased out of the room, which was so different from the meticulous order throughout the rest of the house.

Mary had always said she didn't have time for herself because she had too much to do taking care of the three of them, but Tianna had never taken her seriously. She'd thought Mary had been joking, but now she understood the sacrifices Mary had made; Mary didn't have a life of her own.

Tianna crossed the hallway, determined to try harder, and vowing not to argue with Mary anymore, but an eerie humming distracted her.

The soft sound was coming from her own bed-room. She eased to the door and peered inside. A ghostly breeze ruffled the tangle of sheets on her bed and made the lamp shades sway.

In the corner near her CD player, an un-natural darkness swirled. She stepped back, adrenaline surging through her. It definitely wasn't her imagination. Maybe shape-shifting Followers had trailed her after all.

She stood her ground, muscles taut, her power crackling through her. This time she would not run.

CHAPTER THREE

THE DARKNESS CURLED into lazy silhouettes, stirring the string of yellow paper lanterns hanging from Tianna's ceiling. Then the scent of peanut butter and bananas filled the room, and Tianna relaxed, able to make out the faces of Vanessa and Catty in the misty forms.

"You scared me." Tianna walked past her unmade bed, shaking out her arms to release the built-up energy.

"We didn't mean to." Vanessa went in and out of focus, her voice thin and ghostly.

"That's okay," Tianna said, and in playful revenge she brushed her fingers over their phantom shadows. The scattered specks rushed around her hand, frantically pulling back together.

"That tickles!" Giggles broke through Vanessa's words, and Catty laughed, fading back to dots.

Then Vanessa materialized, silver stars glinting on her cheekbones, her eyes smoky with eyeliner. Her blond hair fell in curls over the black crystals glued to her neck, collarbone, and shoulders in dramatic swirls. She stepped forward, a silky bag swinging from her arm, and handed Tianna a peanut-butter cookie. "What are you going to tell Derek?"

"I don't know." Tianna took a bite, and sweetness filled her mouth.

"You don't know?" Catty became solid, her fifties-style cat-eye glasses sparkling. She wore velvet low-slung slacks and had painted a floral design around her belly ring, adding crystals and sequins to make the flowers sparkle. She held cookies and a peeled banana in her hands. "We've been trying to catch you on the phone, but we couldn't wait a second longer."

"*You* couldn't wait," Vanessa corrected. "I wanted to drive over. Do you know how cold we'll get floating home tonight, especially if there's fog?"

"We'll worry about that later." Catty waved her hand dismissively.

"Are you for real?" Vanessa rolled her eyes. "Why doesn't anything ever bother you?"

"Why should it?" Catty asked. "If it gets too cold, I'll just take us back in time, and we'll relive the evening, but this time use your car."

"I wish I could be more like you." Vanessa sighed and pulled a blue bottle from her bag. She sat on the edge of the bed, kicked off her high-heeled sandals, and spread shimmer cream over her bare legs, giving her skin a dewy glow. She handed the bottle to Tianna, then adjusted her black tube dress. "Well? We came over to hear the details."

"You've got to tell us everything," Catty added.

"I told you already." Tianna fell onto her bed. "He asked me if I thought we were ready for sex."

"Just one sentence?" Catty plopped down next to her. "No pleading? That's it?"

"Derek likes to get right to the point." She started to say more, but Catty and Vanessa were looking at her in an odd way. "What?"

"You look . . ." Catty paused as if searching for a word.

"You're always so perfect, but tonight you look even better," Vanessa offered.

Catty nudged her mischievously. "If you have on new makeup, tell us, so we can steal your tricks."

"I don't know. Maybe it's the light." Tianna tried to shrug off their compliments.

"Maybe it's love," Catty teased.

"Thanks." Tianna fell against them, overcome, and hugged them both fiercely, making them laugh. Lately, some of the girls at school had begun to treat her cruelly because they were jealous of her. They had tagged Tianna's locker and trashed her behind her back, but Tianna couldn't help the way she looked, and it wasn't as if she had been trying to compete. "You're the best friends ever."

"We know," Catty answered with mock conceitedness, and then an impish grin overcame her haughty look. "So, what are you going to tell Derek?"

"I don't have a clue." Tianna clutched a pillow and stared at the ceiling. Right now she had more important things on her mind. Should she tell them?

Vanessa touched her arm as if sensing her anxiety. "What's wrong?"

Tianna looked back at her. "This afternoon, when I was walking home, I think I attacked myself. My powers did, anyway."

"What do you mean?" Vanessa asked, concern in her eyes.

Tianna told them about her embarrassing episode of shadowboxing on Melrose Avenue and the odd feeling later that someone had been running beside her.

"Our gifts act up all the time," Catty said

when she had finished. "Vanessa goes in and out of focus just thinking about Michael, and when I drop back into time, I never know for sure where I'll be."

"It's embarrassing for you when your powers mess up," Tianna agreed. "But mine are different. I'm afraid I'm going to hurt someone." She thought of Todd again, and her stomach clenched.

"You must be way stressed out." Catty stuffed the last bite of banana and cookie into her mouth.

"You think that's all it is?" Tianna asked. "Stress?"

"But this isn't like you," Vanessa added. "You have more confidence than anyone. There's something more than Derek upsetting you. No way could his question do this to you."

Tianna swallowed, not sure where to start, but before she could speak, a horn blared outside. "There he is." She shot up and rushed to the window. Derek's blue Ford Escort was parked at the curb. He was already running up the front walk.

He saw her and held up his free hand, with pinky, index finger, and thumb extended, signing *I love you.*

"He's early, as usual." Tianna waved. Seeing him made her feel better.

Catty nudged her. "He's carrying flowers."

"What's the stuff under his arm?" Vanessa asked.

Tianna smiled. "Travel brochures."

Catty and Vanessa looked at her.

"We plan trips together," she explained. "Galapagos, Antarctica, Angkor."

Vanessa shook her head. "Haven't you ever heard of London?"

Tianna shoved her good-humoredly. "Go let him in. I'm not even dressed."

Seconds later, Derek was pacing on the entrance tiles and whistling off-key, the soft tap of his footsteps echoing up the stairs. Catty and Vanessa had left, agreeing to meet up later at Planet Bang.

Tianna snapped crystals into her hair, then

slipped on dangling star earrings. The pattern matched the night sky beaded across her black halter top. Her low-slung, silky skirt was still draped over a hanger on the shower rod. She didn't want to wrinkle it just yet.

She outlined her lips, then filled in color, but when she drew eyeliner over her top lid, she made a jagged line. She opened the medicine cabinet and pulled out a bottle of makeup remover, then slammed the door closed, grabbed a cotton ball and glanced into the mirror.

She sucked in air, startled, and her heart skipped a beat. A young man stood behind her, his face obscured in a pillar of rising smoke. The bottle fell from her hand and shattered on the floor. At the same moment, she whipped around, swinging her leg in a karate kick. Her foot hit air and crashed to the bathroom floor with a hard whack, the sole of her shoe scattering shards of broken glass.

Whoever had been there was gone now. Had it been only a figment of her imagination? With frantic, jagged movements, she turned back and gazed into the mirror again, trying to see what might have created the illusion, but she saw nothing unusual now, only the blue bathroom wall. She closed her eyes, breathing through her mouth, and tried to calm her shaky nerves.

When she looked up again, someone was behind her, reflected in the mirror.

CHAPTER FOUR

TIANNA SPUN AROUND, but this time her heart found a carefree rhythm, and the energy quivering on the tips of her fingers shot over her with an excited glow. Derek stood there, his blue eyes filled with alarm.

"Are you okay?" He glanced at the glass on the floor. "I heard a crash and came up to see what had happened."

She fell against him, absorbing his warmth, his jacket rough against her arms. "I thought I saw someone's reflection in the mirror. It startled me, and I dropped the bottle."

That was what she said, but she didn't think it had been only a slash of darkness on the wall. She had seen a young man's face. Maybe she had a ghost haunting her. If so, what did it want from her?

"No one's here now." Derek's hands glided over her bare back, tender and reassuring.

Tianna looked down at the broken bottle and concentrated, picturing it whole. A low hum buzzed through her, and the fractured glass scraped across the linoleum, forming larger and larger pieces, the spilled liquid swirling along with them. Finally the bottle reassembled, with the fluid sloshing inside. She picked it up and put it back in the medicine cabinet.

"You're amazing," Derek whispered. He knew she was a Daughter and loved to watch her use her power. Two Followers had captured them together, before Tianna had even heard about the Atrox.

Derek glanced down at his watch. "Hurry and get dressed. I want to show you something outside."

With a gasp she remembered that her skirt was still on its hanger. She was standing in her panties and halter top. She blushed and grabbed a towel, whipping it around her waist.

"It's okay." Derek smiled, too broadly. "I've seen you in your swimsuit before."

"This is different," she squealed in exasperation and pushed him from the bathroom. She slammed the door.

"Really, it's all right." His words broke through his laughter.

"All right for you, maybe," she answered back and slipped into her skirt.

Moments later they crossed to the front lawn, the soft fragrance of honeysuckle wafting around them. Her mini clung nicely to her hips. She liked the silky feel against her skin and the tap of her spiky sandals on the walk.

Suddenly, Derek grabbed her and turned her to the east. "There," he said against her ear, his breath warm and sweet.

The full moon rose, glossing palm trees and rooftops with a milky glow. Tianna stretched in the luxurious light. Moonbeams trickled over her like raindrops, but the white luster also brought a deepening sense of foreboding. She drew back, rubbing her arms.

"What's wrong?" Derek asked.

She looked up at him, loving the concern in his eyes, and started to tell him about her session with Madame Oskar, but he spoke before she could.

"Native Americans called this the Full Wolf Moon," he said. "Wolves went hungry in winter and howled at the night sky, complaining about their empty stomachs."

"I don't think we'll see any wolves tonight." She started toward his car, suddenly wanting to dance and forget her problems.

Derek opened the passenger-side door.

She climbed in, her skirt sliding up her thighs, and paused to watch him look at her. The thought of being alone with him made her stomach tighten. What would she tell him? She had kissed him, but never more.

He caught her looking up at him. A dreamy

smile covered his face; then he slammed the car door and ran around to the driver's side. He slipped behind the steering wheel, stuck the key in the ignition, and whispered, "Please start."

The engine stirred with a grating sound.

"Come on. Come on," he coaxed impatiently.

This time, when he turned the key, Tianna willed the car to go. The engine clattered, and they rolled down the street, the dashboard shimmying.

"You really have to get it fixed," she said. "You said it would be a quick repair."

"Quick but expensive. I can't afford it." Derek leaned forward in concentration. He didn't trust the brakes. "I'm saving for our first trip."

Balmy air rushed over Tianna and she leaned back, resting her head on the seat back, wondering what Madame Oskar had seen in her future. Maybe it was something connected to her seventeenth birthday. All Daughters had to make an important decision when they turned seventeen, but did she?

Catty, Vanessa, and Serena talked about the

metamorphosis often. They could either choose to lose their powers and their memories of being goddesses, or they could transform into something else, guardian spirits, perhaps. But Tianna hadn't been born a goddess, so did she have to make a choice? Maggie had never told her.

A loud bang jolted her from her thoughts.

The car backfired again and died a few feet from a parking stall near Planet Bang. Derek bumped his forehead comically on the steering wheel.

"Maybe I can help." Tianna nudged the car into place with a thought.

Minutes later, they walked inside Planet Bang, music pulsing around them. The DJ started another song, and a rainbow of laser lights flitted over the walls. Kids crowded the floor, pressed tightly together, moving with the beat. Tianna started to dance close to Derek. She lifted her arms, loving the feel of his hands on her bare waist.

Derek leaned over her, pulling her closer. "You feel tense tonight." His words brushed against her temple, the caress of his lips stirring something pleasant inside her. "If you're nervous about my question, we'll forget I asked."

She blushed. Where had her cool confidence gone?

"I didn't mean to upset you," he continued.

She closed her eyes and let her arms slip around his neck, then took a deep breath, determined to tell him exactly how she felt. "Derek," she began, "I—"

She broke off, stopped by a sudden feeling that someone was watching her. She whipped around. Corrine stood with her friends Jessica and Melanie, glaring at her with hateful intensity, obviously talking about her.

"What's with them?" Derek put a protective hand on her shoulder. "Corrine used to be so sweet."

Tianna didn't understand why Corrine had turned on her, spreading vicious rumors. They had been friends once.

Now Corrine entered the throng of dancers and shoved toward them, with Melanie and Jessica trailing behind her. Finally they stood beside Tianna, all attitude and peevish stares.

"Cute crystals in your hair," Corrine said, her tone implying the opposite. She had just gotten collagen injections in her lips and was vamped out, with too much gloss.

"I like your style, too." Tianna tried to hold back the words, but her mouth went on automatic. "Isn't that what Vanessa wore last year? Or maybe it was the year before."

"You think you're so much better than everyone." Melanie sneered and struck a pose, her eyes drifting over the dancers. She caught something and nudged Corrine. "There's Katrina."

"Let's go talk to Thunder Thighs." Corrine turned with an air of confidence.

Katrina had spent the winter break at a weight-loss camp, but she still looked chunky.

"Leave her alone," Tianna ordered.

"Why?" Jessica cooed, and straightened her size double-zero dress. "Maybe she'll share her diet tricks."

Something turned inside Tianna. "Don't do it."

"Like you wouldn't?" Corrine eased away.

Tianna glared after her, her energy roused. Sparks flickered off her fingers.

"Tianna," Derek whispered. "You're not supposed to use your power that way."

"Too late," she answered, a savage taste in her mouth. Her power struck, snapping the heels on Corrine's sandals. Corinne tumbled forward. Melanie tried to catch her, but then Tianna snagged Melanie's hemline. Her skirt unraveled, the wad of strings tripping her.

Jessica started to laugh and slapped her hands over her perfect lips, but suddenly her long blond hair frizzed up as if someone had blasted it with a blow-dryer. She shrieked and lost her balance, plummeting onto Melanie.

Kids stopped dancing and watched the girls, but a guy with spiked hair shot Tianna a hostile look. She flinched. He couldn't know she was responsible for their falling, but he stared at her accusingly and helped Corrine stand. Who was he?

Jimena appeared from the crowd and tilted her head, smiling, her long black hair all glitter and curls. "I guess you got Corrine hooked up with this month's heartthrob."

"You know him?" Tianna asked.

Corrine had recovered from her fall and was dancing barefoot around the good-looking guy, her body brushing against his; he kept glancing at Tianna.

"*Claro que sí*. Every girl does. He's in my biology class," Jimena explained. Iridescent purple shadow shimmered around her eyes; her two teardrop tattoos sparkled with silver. Her slacks were tight and sexy-low, revealing old gang markings across her stomach.

"Did you get any new memories back?" Tianna asked.

"*Muy pocos*." Jimena nodded with frustration. "Only a few. We need to talk. I've got bad news."

Tianna reluctantly pulled away from Derek and headed after Jimena, threading her way through the kids jammed near the back.

Jimena had turned seventeen already and had chosen to give up her powers, but when she lost her memories of being a Daughter of the Moon, other recollections of past lives had come back to her with startling clarity. She was the reincarnation of the ancient goddess Pandia, the daughter of Selene and Zeus. She had come back to earth many times, but she couldn't yet remember her purpose for this return. She only knew she needed to help the Daughters prevent a catastrophic event.

Tianna stepped outside and felt a sudden chill. A breeze had come in from the ocean, bringing cool air and mist. Serena, Vanessa, and Catty stood huddled beneath a heat lamp in front of a new Vietnamese restaurant. Jimena and Tianna joined them. The smell of fresh herbs floated from the tables of the diners eating on the patio.

"I don't think we want to hear this," Serena said as if she had already pushed into Jimena's mind and caught her thoughts. She wore an off-the-shoulder tee showing off the moon and stars painted on her arm and accented with blue crystals. Her tongue ring clicked against her teeth.

"What do you need to tell us?" Vanessa asked, playing nervously with her amulet.

"The Atrox broke its binding and it's more dangerous now," Jimena said matter-of-factly.

"More?" Catty tilted her head, and her nose stud caught the light. "How can it be more dangerous than it was before?"

"Because it can take human form again," Jimena answered, cautiously examining the darkness beneath the bougainvillea.

"Again?" Tianna felt puzzled. "Did it ever?"

"When Maggie was a young girl in ancient Greece," Jimena said, speaking slowly, as if recalling Maggie made her sad, "it often appeared as a man until Maggie bound it to its shadow, but over the centuries the binding has weakened, and now it has freed itself."

"So it could be any man we see?" Vanessa asked.

"Or girl, woman, child," Jimena continued. "It can even appear as an animal, and that makes it more treacherous."

"But as a person, wouldn't it be more vulnerable?" Catty asked.

Serena shook her head, her dark hair sleek

and shining. "A strange black cloud makes anyone suspicious, but no one would run from a crying child or an injured dog."

Tianna stared at Serena, wondering if she knew more. After all, she was in love with Stanton, a Follower. Their relationship had once been forbidden, but now that he had become the Prince of Night, nothing was denied him. Unlike the others, when Serena turned seventeen she had a third choice: she could become a goddess of the dark. Tianna wondered if she had already become one. Serena had said more than once that she felt a spiritual connection to Hekate and wanted to become one of the *mysticae*, who were initiated into the secret rites of the goddess, because she understood the purpose of the dark now.

"We need to shackle it to its shadow again," Jimena said, interrupting Tianna's thoughts. "So it can only appear to others in its supernatural form."

Vanessa looked mystified. "How can we tie it to its shadow? I mean, a shadow slips through your fingers. It's not solid."

"We need to find the sword Maggie used before," Jimena explained.

"A sword?" Serena looked surprised. "Stanton has been trying to find a sword."

"Why does he want it?" Jimena asked. Her eyes flashed, and then she and Serena stared at each other as if a telepathic conversation were passing between them.

"He probably wants to destroy it," Catty put in, not bothering to hide her accusation. "We'd better find it first."

Serena turned on her. "I can't believe you still don't trust Stanton. Why do you always think he's going to do something to hurt us?" Serena frowned and folded her arms over her chest, her bracelets jingling. "Don't bother to answer my question. I caught your thoughts. Someday you'll know Stanton isn't who you think."

"He's next in line to the Atrox," Vanessa said in frustration, defending Catty.

"Maybe this is the reason you came down to earth," Tianna broke in, speaking to Jimena. "To help us bind the Atrox again."

But Jimena shook her head. Her gaze was distant. "The four of you could do the binding without my help. There's something worse coming, and it's approaching rapidly."

CHAPTER FIVE

TIANNA'S MOON AMULET began to glow. She nudged Catty, and the others became silent, their charms casting eerie, white light over their faces. A strange, ebony shadow glided beneath a nearby bougainvillea, eclipsing the normal darkness of night. Then a sudden slash of black swept through the overhanging blossoms, and a cloudburst of flowers showered over them.

Serena smiled and picked up a fuchsia petal. "Is that all, then?"

Tianna relaxed, knowing that Stanton had created the alarm.

"We can't do anything until we know more." Jimena brushed flowers from her hair and then touched the Medusa stone hanging around her neck. She no longer wore a moon amulet. The snakes in the hair of the woman in the cameo writhed around each other.

Tianna had gotten used to seeing the sinuous motion, but now she wondered if it meant anything.

Jimena shot Serena a warning look. "We might as well go back inside," she said, and started up the street. "¡Vamos!"

"I'll catch you later." Serena ignored her and went the other way. She hurried down a path beside the restaurant, her sandals tapping on gray stones. When she reached the trellis, the velvet dark swept around her, and Stanton materialized, his arms already cradling her. He looked like any high-school guy, with blond hair and a gold stud earring, but then his eyes caught the moonlight and shone yellow.

A chill crept up Tianna's back, and her skin prickled with goose bumps. She didn't understand why Serena didn't feel Stanton's sinister aura. Sometimes she even felt as if she could detect an odd scent about him, something too sweet and clean. She wondered vaguely if evil had an odor.

Serena kissed him, and then they dissolved into swirling smoke and rose into the night.

"I hope she's careful." Catty shook her head and watched the vapor soaring over the buildings.

Vanessa nodded. Her black tube dress had slipped low, revealing the edge of the arabesque tattoo over her heart. The black crystals on her neck sparkled. "Jimena said Serena has even been cutting classes to be with him."

"I don't understand why she can't feel his evil." Tianna frowned, but her mind quickly shifted to other problems. She glanced in the opposite direction, wishing Jimena would come back and tell them more, but she had already gone inside the club.

"Let's go," Vanessa started back. "I've got to be onstage in a few minutes. Michael's band has already started to play."

Catty followed after her, but Tianna waited

under the heat lamp. She had new worries to consider now.

"Aren't you coming, Tianna?" Catty asked, looking back over her shoulder.

Tianna shook her head, her stomach knotting with distress.

Catty obviously misunderstood her look. She nodded with an impish grin. "I'll tell Derek you're waiting outside." She ran past Vanessa as if she were Cupid on a mission. When she reached the entrance, she turned and yelled back, "See you tomorrow, and I want details!"

She and Vanessa ducked inside.

Tianna walked over to Derek's car and started to shiver, certain it wasn't just from the cold. Maybe she was the one responsible for weakening the Atrox's binding. Jimena had said it was due only to the passage of time, but Tianna wasn't convinced. Months back she had found the Secret Scroll at Catty's house and had foolishly used it to summon the Atrox, believing she could destroy it. Could she have unwittingly spoken an incantation that had helped it escape?

Laughter interrupted her thoughts. The guy with the spiked hair who had shot her a hostile look inside came out the emergency exit, bringing the unmistakable sound of Michael's music with him. The riffs sounded like a locomotive at high speed. The door shut and the guitar chords became distant thunder again, more vibration than melody.

Corrine walked beside the cute-looking guy. She was curled under his arm like the queen of cool. When she caught Tianna's gaze, she clutched his side, as if showing off a trophy, and giggled. They ambled away, heads together, sharing secrets.

Soon after, footsteps pounded down the sidewalk behind her. Tianna turned, and Derek joined her. He put his arm around her shoulders. "What's up?"

She leaned against his chest, grateful for his warmth. "Could you take me home?"

"Sure." He placed his hand on her waist, his fingers stroking her bare skin.

Immediately she realized her mistake. She

didn't need to be a mind reader to know he thought she wanted to leave early for another reason. What was she going to tell him now?

"I just want to go back to my house," she tried to explain.

"I know. No one will be home." He grinned broadly and opened the car door. The hinges protested with an irritating grate.

Tianna slid in and buckled her seatbelt in place. "I really mean I just want to go home."

But Derek was already running around the front of the car and clearly hadn't heard her. She let out a sigh. This day could not possibly get more messed up.

Derek climbed behind the wheel and turned the key in the ignition. The engine clunked, then roared, shooting black smoke into the air. He pulled away and shot down the street.

Minutes later, Derek steered the car toward the curb in front of her home. It coasted to a stop beneath the street lamp. The wind had picked up, bending the trees, making their shadows swarm like phantoms back and forth across the windshield.

Derek turned slowly and looked at her, his eyes intense. He eased his hand over the backseat. He seemed more handsome than ever, his smile more beguiling. Her stomach fluttered. How many times had she fantasized about going farther than a kiss? But now her body prickled with anxiety, not desire. She tried to swallow and her throat tightened. "I'd better go in."

"In a minute." He unsnapped her seatbelt and drew her to him. His fingers brushed over her cheek as if he understood her nervousness. He gently turned her head until she was gazing into his eyes. Then he kissed her and pulled back, his breath soft and warm on her face. "I love you, Tianna. Forever."

Her lips parted and he bent to kiss her again.

"Let's go up to your room," he whispered.

From the corner of her eye she caught a sudden movement, not a spectral shade this time. Someone was standing outside the car, watching them.

CHAPTER SIX

IANNA WRENCHED HER head around and accidentally hit Derek's jaw. Her heart hammered hard, but now she didn't see anyone standing by the front fender. Still, she felt certain the figure hadn't been her imagination.

"Ouch!" Derek winced and jerked back, grabbing his chin.

"Sorry," she answered, but it was a quick throwaway remark. Her attention remained focused on the shadows slipping back and forth between the trees.

"Dang, Tianna." Derek had too much accusation in his voice. "If you didn't want to do anything, all you had to do was say no. It wasn't like I was forcing you."

She ignored him and clasped her amulet. It lay cold in her palm, but she sensed danger, something in the night that didn't belong. What had she seen?

Mist slipped in from the ocean, twining around the chimney and reflecting the moonlight with an eerie, spectral glow. The vapors shrouded treetops and the wind murmured through the leaves, churning the fog. Palm fronds rustled near a dim streetlamp, but their swaying wasn't enough to have caused the silhouette.

She sat motionless, barely breathing, holding her energy tight. Her power purred through her, poised, and then, slowly, she became aware of Derek talking to her.

"I think you chipped my tooth." He craned his neck to study his teeth in the rearview mirror.

"I didn't do it on purpose," she whispered angrily, her eyes vigilant. "If I had wanted to push you off me, don't you think I could have done it another way?"

To prove her point she let go. The car filled with a soft whooshing sound, and an unseen pressure pushed Derek back in his seat. His eyes widened and he shot her a quizzical look, shocked, and caught his breath.

"I thought I saw someone standing by the car," she explained.

A ripple of murky shadow near the house made her look again. If anything had been there, it was gone now.

"I shouldn't have gotten so upset," he apologized, his good humor returning. "I never felt your power before. It feels so cool, like invisible hands—"

"Like hands?" she asked, suddenly more interested in what he had to say than the dark tracing across the lawn.

He nodded. "When you shoved me back, it felt like real, honest-to-goodness hands pressing against my chest."

She stared at him, certain now that her own

telekinesis explained the feeling of someone grabbing her earlier in the day. That solved one mystery, and maybe a sudden gust did account for the figure she had seen near the car. If her nerves hadn't been on edge, she probably wouldn't even have noticed the change in light. That left only the young man she had seen reflected in the bathroom mirror. She rubbed her temples. Had she only imagined him, too?

"I'm sorry, Derek, so sorry," Tianna said. "I've been really stressed. My powers have been out of control, and I just have too much on my mind."

"You're always worrying lately. That's not like you." Derek grasped her shoulder and pulled her tenderly to him. "Can't you just relax? Be your old self?"

"I've tried," she said and cuddled against him.

"I hope I didn't upset you, but I thought when you wanted to leave Planet Bang early, you were telling me yes. I mean what was I supposed to think after that e-mail you sent me?"

"What e-mail?" Tianna asked. She couldn't recall having sent him one.

"You know, about taking things beyond what we were doing. You were pretty graphic. It didn't seem like you. That's why I asked if you thought we were ready to have sex."

"Corrine!" Tianna wanted to spit. "What's with her?"

"You didn't send the e-mail?" Derek sounded disappointed.

She tilted her head and raised one eyebrow. "Do you really think I would have discussed *that* in an e-mail? Corrine probably sent it out to everyone in her address book. I wouldn't be surprised." Tianna shook her head, imagining the looks she was going to get at school on Monday.

"I guess I knew, but I was hoping." He smiled sheepishly, then added, "What did you do to Corrine to make her go on such a rampage against you?"

Tianna shook her head. "She was my first friend at school when I transferred in. Maybe she got upset when I started hanging out with Catty." She opened the car door. "I'd better go. I've got the skateboard competition tomorrow."

"I wish I could go watch you, but I have to work." He started to get out.

"I can walk myself up to the door." She climbed out, not waiting for him.

He leaned over and looked up at her. "I'll pick you up for Jessica's party tomorrow. Eight okay?"

She nodded. "Sounds good."

"Are you sure you want to go?" he asked. "I mean, the way Corrine and Jessica acted. . . ."

"It's a party. Of course I want to go. Besides, if I don't show up, Jessica and Corrine will think they've gotten to me, and they'll only torment me more." She slammed the door.

He waved and the car barreled down the street, leaving a trail of black smoke. Derek turned the corner too quickly and the hubcap scraped against the curb, spraying sparks.

Tianna smiled, knowing he was trying to get home before the car broke down completely.

She started up the walk, opening her small silk shoulder bag. She pulled out her keys and paused. A deeper shadow waited near the door.

She suddenly wished she had left the porch light on. She stepped cautiously forward, straining to see.

Whatever it was moved toward her, and then Madame Oskar stepped from the dark, her scarves fluttering behind her. Dangling coins on her belt glistened in the moonlight, and her face, without theatrical makeup, looked delicate. Her black hair, free of her usual turban, flowed to her waist.

Tianna stepped backward, shocked. "How did you know where I live?"

"You gave me your address." Madame spoke in hushed tones, then rummaged through a pocket and brought out the pink information sheet Tianna had filled out for the mailing list. "I had my daughter follow you in case you had lied on the card."

Tianna nodded, wondering if that explained the odd feeling she'd had that someone had been following her on Melrose Avenue. She stared at Madame, perturbed. "Why did you need to know where I live?"

"I was concerned about you." Madame Oskar said. "You were so frightened today."

"You startled me," Tianna agreed. "Breaking the crystal ball was a bit dramatic, don't you think? Why did you throw it at the wall, anyway?"

"I didn't," Madame explained. "I was trying to catch it."

"I saw you hurl it at the wall," Tianna insisted.

"Why would I destroy such a beautiful globe?" Madame argued. "It's been in my family for years. It was you. When the clouds uncovered your future, you became upset and threw it."

"How could I?" Tianna stuck her key in the lock. She wanted to go inside, make popcorn, watch TV, and forget about this day and night. "I didn't even touch it."

"You used your power," Madame said quietly, then added in a harsh whisper. "I know what you are."

Tianna tapped her finger nervously on the doorknob. "What am I, then?"

Madame started to speak, but something in the sky caught her attention.

Tianna wondered what she was seeing. Madame edged deeper onto the porch, closer to Tianna again.

"Fortune-telling can only predict what might happen," she said hurriedly, whispering, as if other forces were listening.

"What you do is a trick?" Tianna countered, suddenly tired and no longer willing to listen. "You can't really see the future?"

"Only God can know what *will* happen," Madame said, the urgency in her voice growing. "The future I see in the crystal ball is never fixed, even when it is ordained by the Atrox."

Tianna's breath caught. "You know about the Atrox?" Her heart thudded heavily, as if saying the name could summon it. "How do you know about the Atrox?"

"I am a half-blood Romani, a *poshrat*," she explained.

"A what?" Tianna asked, wondering if she were some kind of Follower, or maybe a Renegade.

"A gypsy," Madame Oskar said, obviously annoyed with Tianna's lack of knowledge. "My people left India centuries ago, because a dark force was threatening us. Now I see that same sinister power trying to take over your life."

"Is that what you saw in my future?" Tianna asked, beginning to relax. Such a threat was not new. The Atrox was forever trying to destroy the Daughters. "I'll survive."

Madame stepped off the porch, her footsteps silent. "We create our own futures. What you and I saw is only a warning of what is probable."

"I didn't see anything," Tianna assured her.

"Some part of you did," Madame argued. "Because you threw my crystal ball."

Tianna started to protest, but Madame continued, "Your destiny can be changed. Each small decision you make can alter what was meant to be."

Madame Oskar held out her hand, the fingers long and slender and heavy with gold rings that looked ancient. "That's why I've come to offer you a chance. Come with me."

"Now? Tonight?" Tianna felt confused. "Where?"

"We'll go until we feel safe. I'll protect you. My people will."

"From the Atrox?" Tianna asked.

"No," Madame answered bluntly. "We'll protect you from yourself."

This was not the answer Tianna had expected; suddenly her mistrust fell away, replaced by an acute need to know. "What did you see in that crystal ball?"

A sudden flash of darkness streaked across the misty sky like a bolt of black lightning.

Madame put her hands up as if protecting herself. "I have no time to explain now. We must leave." She offered her hand to Tianna again but continued walking backward. "Come with me."

Tianna didn't budge.

Madame turned and ran swiftly down the sidewalk. At the street she looked back at Tianna, contempt on her face, then marked the air with her fingers, as if she were sending a curse.

The engine grumbled in the van behind her, and when Madame climbed in, the dome light came on, revealing four people waiting inside. As the van pulled away from the curb, headlights flashed on up and down the street. Trucks and cars that had appeared empty were crowded with men, women, and children. One by one the vehicles pulled into the road and the caravan headed away.

Tianna watched, wondering what terror Madame Oskar had seen that could have made her community leave Los Angeles.

Suddenly Tianna needed to be inside the safety of her home. She unlocked the door and hurried in, slamming the door behind her. She flicked on the light switch, and someone grabbed her hand.

CHAPTER SEVEN

"STRANGE VISITORS." Stanton brushed his shaggy blond bangs from his eyes and smiled sensually. "Do carloads of people often drop by to curse you?"

"Where's Serena?" Tianna's body became alert, poised to run. She wasn't afraid yet, but his evil aura made her shrink back. Her amulet thrummed against her chest. She eased her hand behind her, searching for the doorknob.

"She didn't come with me," he said at last. "And I don't want her to know I was here."

"I can't keep this a secret from her." Tianna

tried not to look, but it was hard not to stare. His dangerous eyes reminded her of impossibly blue skies, long summer days filled with . . . She shook her head. He was hypnotizing her.

"You'll keep our meeting secret," he ordered, and there was something more than threat in his voice. She felt him in her mind now, like a cool rush of blood to her head.

She willed her powers to grow, but her energy only scattered in aimless flashes about her, disorganized, her mind too muddled to concentrate. Sparks sprinkled over his face, landing in a nest of stars on his jaw.

Her chaotic display didn't frighten Stanton. He seemed amused. He placed a hand on the wall above her and leaned down, his body uncomfortably close. "I didn't mean to startle you."

"So you were the one watching Derek and me?" She tried to sound bold, but a tremor broke through her words.

"Why would I do that?" he asked in a teasing tone. "What would I have seen? Anything interesting?"

Heat rose to her cheeks, a blush betraying her embarrassment. She struggled to hide her thoughts about Derek.

Stanton grinned mischievously, and she knew he had caught every lusty daydream she'd ever had.

"So why did you tell him you didn't want to have sex?" Stanton leaned closer. "When obviously—"

"I didn't lie." She started to defend herself but then stopped. By some odd transference of thought, she caught Stanton carefully examining her memory of the silhouette she had glimpsed by the car's front fender. Why would that interest him?

He pulled away, his eyes concerned. "You need to be more cautious," he said simply.

"Why do you care what happens to me?" And in a flash, she knew. If something bad happened in her future, Serena could be in danger. She was the one he was trying to protect. What made him so devoted to a Daughter? Surely it was because Serena was the key, able to alter the balance between light and dark forces.

"I do it because I love Serena," he said, answering her thoughts.

"Then, tell me, what is going to happen?" she asked, hating the jagged fear that had crept into her body.

"I don't see the future, if that's what you mean, but everyone is talking about you." He brushed a hand over her cheek. "All the Followers are."

His touch made her flinch.

"I can taste your fear," he said, close enough to kiss her. "But you shouldn't be afraid of me." His finger traced down her neck, and she could feel his breath ruffling through her hair. "Do you think I've come here to harm you?"

"I don't know." Her energy fluttered, and spangled light shot from her, but did nothing to push him away. Was he controlling her powers, too?

"You're so incredibly beautiful," he said, with unbearable sadness.

"Thank you." She gulped. Did Followers two-time their girlfriends? Was that what this was about? "I like Derek—" She started to let him down easy, but he interrupted her with a hearty laugh.

"That's not what I'm after." Then sorrow returned to his face. "I'm sorry, Tianna," he whispered, his eyes entrancing. "So terribly sorry."

"About what?"

"You really don't know, do you?" he asked. "I thought staying here would have brought some memories back and you'd want to talk."

She stared at him, fascinated and repelled. "Why would I ever want to talk to you?"

"I know you hate me almost as much as you despise the Atrox," he said in a hushed tone. "But I don't want you to be afraid to come to me. In the future I may be the only person you can trust."

Even in her half-conscious state, she caught the absurdity of what he was saying. "That's impossible. I'd never trust you over the Daughters." She started to laugh but stopped. He was dead serious.

"What if they were gone?" he asked simply. "Who could you turn to then?"

"Is that what you see in my future?" she asked, her heart lurching; but then, through her daze another thought came to her. Stanton was a master of deceit, and she had almost fallen for his ploy. What did he want from her, really? She didn't trust him. She never would.

A sudden rumbling made him pull back.

"It's the garage door opening," Tianna explained, anxious for him to leave. "I'll get in trouble if Mary sees you here. She has this thing about guys visiting." That's what she said, but secretly she worried he might harm Mary or Shannon.

An insolent grin crossed his face. He made no move to leave. "I haven't come here to harm anyone. I'd like to meet your mother."

Footsteps sounded across the linoleum in the kitchen.

"Tianna!" Shannon's voice echoed through the house.

"Can't you just blast what you need to tell me into my brain and go?" Tianna pleaded, hating the whimpering tone in her voice.

He folded his arms across his chest. "I'd like to spend an evening watching TV with you and your family. Do you have some microwave popcorn?"

She groaned in frustration.

The kitchen door swung open and Shannon slammed into the living room, a purple bandage tight around the crook of her arm, a rosary clutched in her hand. "I get to stay home tonight!"

"Great!" Tianna rushed to greet her, still wondering how she was going to explain Stanton.

Shannon fell into her arms and they hugged, rocking back and forth. Mary followed after her, an odd look on her face.

"I can explain," Tianna said, searching her mind for a lie to cover Stanton's presence in their home.

CHAPTER EIGHT

"AN EXPLANATION FOR what, dear?" Mary set her leather purse on the couch. Her pink suit jacket was speckled with what might have been dried chocolate, vomit, or blood. Her eyes looked tired and she had lost an earring.

"I wanted—" Tianna glanced behind her, ready to introduce Stanton and bear the consequences, but he had left. A shadow spread over the wall like a smear of gray soot, then slipped away. The door jiggled as if Stanton were saying good-bye.

"Nothing," Tianna said, rubbing her chest to quiet her heart. "It wasn't important."

Mary cupped Tianna's chin in her palm and studied her face. "You haven't been taking your vitamins."

"I accidentally dropped them on the floor," Tianna lied. When was Mary going to figure out that she never took the vitamins? Then her eyes fixed on Mary's hairline. How had she not noticed the wig before? Had she been that self-absorbed? It was so obvious to her now.

"I'll fix you a veggie drink." Mary breezed away, plucking at her hair.

Shannon stuck her finger in her mouth. "That stuff is so gross. I hate the one she makes for me with the broccoli." She slipped the rosary around her neck and followed Tianna into the kitchen. "I hope she doesn't make me drink one. I'll barf if she does."

Mary was already at the counter, cutting herbs from a planter. She tossed the green sprigs into a blender, then added a fishy-smelling brown liquid and milk. She pressed a speed-control button and the motor whirred. Then she wiped her hands on the back of her skirt, leaving stains, and grabbed a glass.

"Why don't you kick off your shoes?" Tianna asked, staring at her pointed pumps. "Those shoes look like real toe-pinchers."

An odd smile crossed Mary's face. "That's a curious thing to say." She stepped out of her shoes, wiggled her perfectly manicured toes, and switched off the blender.

Tianna wondered briefly if the red marks on the carpet upstairs had come from the paint-by-numbers sets or from nail polish.

Shannon opened the refrigerator and took out a Coke. She popped the tab, but before she could take a sip, Mary took the can and replaced it with a bottle of water. Then she handed Tianna the glass filled with frothing sludge.

"Maybe Shannon could sleep in my room tonight," Tianna suggested. "So you don't have to stay up with her."

A look of gratitude flashed across Mary's weary face. "I suppose. Shannon?"

"Great." Shannon opened the bottled water. "Can we mess around with your makeup?"

"Sure." Tianna nodded, held her breath and swallowed. The liquid burned down her throat and through her stomach. When she finished, she set the glass down, and sweat beaded on her forehead. It was the first time she had drunk the health drink, and it was definitely going to be her last. "What is in that?"

"Nutrition." Mary laughed. "You need strong bones."

Tianna and Shannon exchanged glances, then darted from the kitchen and ran upstairs to the bedroom.

Hours later Shannon fell asleep on Tianna's bed, vamped out in too much eye makeup. Glitter and hearts adorned her cheeks, and ankle bracelets jingled each time she moved her foot. The room smelled of raspberry cologne, lotion, and fingernail polish.

Tianna paced at the foot of the bed. The urge to run was unrelenting. Maybe she should just go. Pack up and leave that night. So why did she stay? What was the difference this time? It was as if another, stronger, force restrained her, and then she looked down at Shannon sleeping peacefully and understood. She didn't want to leave. This was her home, her family.

She slipped into her pajamas and cuddled next to Shannon, using one of her teddy bears for a pillow. She clutched her moon amulet and prayed for the nightmares to stay away, but the dream came quickly, and in the reverie she had an overpowering need to stargaze. Still asleep, she climbed from bed and went to her window.

A pack of wolves paced on the lawn below. The full moon's glow made their fur gleam with diamond luster. Their long bushy tails, tipped with black, flicked back and forth. The wolves whined and whimpered, pawing at the earth, calling to her.

Suddenly, the smallest one yelped. Another growled, and then the largest let out a volley of sharp barks before releasing a long howl, its snout to the sky. Its cry rose and fell, the eerie sound filling Tianna's heart with an odd longing.

When the first one finished, another took up the cry, beautiful and haunting in its lament. The howling continued unbroken, each song more sorrowful than the last.

Then, unexpectedly, a young man walked into the pack, his face hidden beneath a fedora.

She couldn't see who he was, but she desperately wanted to be with him. She opened her window, and a cold wind rushed over her. She pushed against the screen, then tried to rip it from the frame. The wire mesh held. She tried to summon her power, but in this dreamworld her energy betrayed her and didn't grow.

"Here!" she yelled to the young man. "Look up so I can see your face."

But he walked away, the wolves bounding around him.

"Don't leave me!" she screamed.

The sound of her own voice startled her awake. She stood at the window, her hands pressed against the screen, fingernails broken and bleeding.

"Tianna?"

She spun around.

"Are you all right?" Shannon leaned against the window frame, eyes wide, staring at her, her rosary tight in her fist. "Who was that guy with the dogs?"

"You saw him?" Tianna's heart raced, her mind sliding into panic. "You saw him in your dream?"

"Who could sleep with all that barking?" Shannon said. "Doesn't that guy know there's a leash law in this city? You're probably not allowed to have so many dogs, anyway."

Tianna looked at Shannon, not sure what to tell her, because she didn't know who the guy was herself. She felt jittery and faint. It had to have been a nightmare and this only a continuation of the dream.

"He's just someone from school," she said at last, rubbing her arms against the cold.

"Hmmm." Shannon traipsed back to bed, snuggled under the covers and started to drift off again.

Tianna stared out the window for a long

time. The yard and street were empty now, but the tracks across the dew-wet grass were clearly visible. Now she wondered about the other dreams. Had those nighttime wanderings been real?

CHAPTER NINE

SUNLIGHT STREAKED through the windows, absorbing Tianna's uneasiness and causing the dream from the night before to fade into distant memory. She bolted down the stairs, excitement rushing through her. The competition was today. She burst into the kitchen, carrying her new skateboard, and breathed in the zesty aroma of sausages and muffins.

"Good morning." Mary stood at the stove, watching the news on the small counter TV, commentators droning over the sizzle of frying meat.

"Everything smells great." Tianna set her board down and grabbed a sausage draining on a paper towel. It burned the tips of her fingers, but she shoved it into her mouth anyway and relished the spicy taste. "I'm starved."

Shannon sat in the breakfast nook behind the bouquet of daffodils Derek had given Tianna the night before. A sketch pad lay beside her plate, pencils and charcoals scattered across the white linen tablecloth.

"You okay?" Tianna squeezed in beside her.

"Tired." Shannon flicked bits of eraser from her drawing with the side of her hand.

"You have a real talent for drawing." Tianna stared at the sketch of German shepherds in moonlight, then glanced at the dried blood around her own fingernails. She'd done some weird sleepwalking last night. She wondered what guy in the neighborhood had so many dogs. Whoever it was probably thought she was a real psycho case, the way she'd tried to push out her window screen. She wished she could remember what she had been yelling at him. No wonder he had turned and walked away.

"I made your favorite." Mary interrupted her

thoughts and set a basket filled with steaming blueberry muffins on the table.

"Thanks." Tianna tore one open, then cut a slab of butter and let it melt before taking a bite. A revolting, fishy taste filled her mouth.

"I mixed your vitamins and energy drink into the batter," Mary said proudly and placed a cup of tea with milk in front of Tianna. "I thought it might be an easier way for you to take them."

"What is with all this nutrition?" Tianna asked, anger spiking inside her. Then she remembered Mary's room and her sacrifice, and she pulled back, posing her question another way. "I was wondering why it's so important for me to take so many vitamins. I mean, I feel healthy."

"It's good for you, of course. What other reason could there be?" Mary walked back to the stove and took the skillet off the flame.

Tianna spit the mushy bite of muffin into her napkin and folded it into her lap.

"She made banana muffins for me," Shannon whispered with a sly smile and opened her red pencil box. A muffin was squished inside. "It tastes like cat food."

"How do you know what cat food tastes like?" Tianna teased.

Shannon giggled.

"Are you going shopping with us this morning?" Mary asked, joining them in the breakfast nook.

"I've got the skateboard competition." Tianna jumped up, opened the refrigerator, and chugged milk from the carton.

"You can't go," Mary said quietly behind her.

Tianna set the carton down with a thump and wiped at the milk running down her chin. "What?" She slammed the refrigerator, rattling the cookie jar on top.

"I've changed my mind." Mary said simply.

"But I've already registered." Tianna picked up her skateboard, determined.

Mary stood with deliberate slowness and stepped in front of her, an unpleasantness in her eyes. "I have two children who make daily trips to the hospital, and I don't need a third."

"*One* makes trips," Shannon corrected with an odd bitterness. "One is *in* the hospital."

"I'll wear my helmet and pads," Tianna pleaded. "I always do."

"You can still meet your friends, but you can't compete. My decision is final." She held out her hand. "Give me your skateboard."

Tianna reluctantly surrendered her board and left the kitchen, banging through the swinging door. She crossed the living room, aware of Mary's footsteps close behind her.

At the front door Tianna picked up her backpack, helmet, and pads. If Mary thought it odd that Tianna was taking her gear, she didn't say so.

"Don't be upset." Mary touched her shoulder. "I don't want you to leave angry."

"I understand." Tianna turned, replicating Mary's tight smile. "You're doing it for my own good."

"I watched the videotape Derek made of your skating," Mary explained.

Tianna's heart sank. She had never meant for

Mary to see it. She had thought she had hidden it under her bed, but she must have left it in the VCR. She didn't think Mary would have taken it from her room.

"If you had fallen on those concrete steps—" Mary stopped, as if the accident she envisioned made her ill; then she went on. "You weren't wearing a helmet or pads. Why do you take such risks?"

Tianna shook her head as if she didn't know, but she understood too well. She loved the rush of adrenaline, the control over her body, the awe on the faces of her friends, the vibration of the wheels quivering beneath her shoes, the wind, everything. She could have given a thousand reasons, but instead she simply said, "I'm sorry."

Mary nodded, satisfied, and embraced her, her arms warm and tender. "Now, have fun with your friends but promise, no skating."

"I promise." Tianna slipped outside and waited until Mary had closed the door. Then she picked up another skateboard leaning against the porch rail.

Mary wasn't very observant. Tianna had more than one board. Or maybe she was just too trusting to suspect that Tianna would ever defy her.

Tianna felt a twinge of remorse, but not enough to stop her from competing. She was determined to ride the fire. Besides, Mary's worries were foolish. What could happen?

CHAPTER TEN

AN HOUR LATER, Tianna stared up at the audience, the sun hot on her shoulders and head. For once, more spectators than judges crowded the stands. Vanessa, Serena, and Catty whooped and waved. All three wore sunglasses and bucket caps.

The announcer called Tianna's number and name. Her lips burned, chapped from licking them too much, and her mouth felt dry from nerves. She stepped forward, all attitude, knowing it impressed the fans, and waved. She shot the crowd a confident smile, then tucked her hair into her helmet, adjusted her pads, and stared at the pit in front of her. It looked like a huge, empty swimming pool, the sides impossibly steep.

Rock music blasted from the speakers, pounding through her, and then she ripped, eager to defy gravity. She launched off the edge of the mammoth bowl and hit concrete, the impact jarring up her spin.

Then the magic happened. The vibration of the wheels shimmied through her, becoming part of her and flowing into her blood. Her shoes melded with the board, her feet, legs, and arms easily maneuvering it wherever she wanted to go.

She did a sweeper to warm up, then a handstand kick flip, and the crowd roared. She chucked a three-sixty on the side and was ready to bust out more moves when a strange feeling made her scan the crowd—something she never did, but the impulse overrode her common sense. She blinked, her eyes burning from the sun, and caught a glimpse of Justin and Mason, the Followers who had killed her parents and her younger sister, Jamie.

Adrenaline shot through her. She clutched the side of the board just in time, then hammered down the ramp. Had she really seen them, or had it only been an illusion caused by speed and glaring light?

She swung upward again and tried to focus on her next move, but her mind was spinning, reliving the pain and years spent running from Justin and Mason. Tianna fixed her eyes on the top of the ramp and did a quick invert, not the trick she had planned. She swept down again, her concentration gone, the wheels rattling, no longer smooth.

The sun seemed to fade as more dark memories flashed through her mind. That first night she had run through the woodlot behind her home, the moonbeams flowing through the tree branches like soft fingers guiding her away. She had slept in a pile of trash, and that morning began the days and months of foster placement, the visits with therapists, the countless inquiries from social workers. More than anything she had wanted a home again, but always an intuitive force had told her it was time to move on. Now she wondered if Mason and Justin were the reason she had been feeling the urge to run again.

She sensed the tension rising in the audience and slammed back to the present. She flew up the ramp, propelled into the air, but she had hesitated one second too long. She grabbed the board with her back hand and tried to plant the other on the ledge, but her fingers jammed against the edge, scraping off a line of skin.

The audience seemed to suck in air and let it out in a collective groan, anticipating her fall.

She desperately tried to reclaim her balance, but it was too late. She had lost her concentration and speed. She could use her telekinetic gift to ease over the lip but that was worse than cheating.

Her neck twisted, her feet slipped, and gravity won. She stared at the gray concrete eight feet below.

CHAPTER ELEVEN

TIANNA HIT THE RAMP hard, bounced once, then smacked against the concrete again. Pain shattered through her. Her elbow slammed down, the pad absorbing the bone-breaking blow; she was going to have major bruises on her hand, arm, and side.

Her board clattered beside her and she slid to a stop, the sunlight glaring in her eyes.

The audience moaned, and the music went silent. She tried to sit up, but her back was racked with misery. She lay stone-still, catching her breath and gathering her strength. She closed her eyes, vowing to never disobey Mary again. Now she wondered if Mary's concern had been based on some kind of maternal premonition.

Running footsteps pounded the ground. She turned her head, ignoring the ache, and glanced up. Two paramedics sprinted toward her. A red case sat on the gurney they were rolling at her. No way were they carrying her out. She got up on her hands and knees, ignoring the soreness, then stood, limped over to her board, and bent, self-conscious about her stiff movement, and with an agonizing stretch, she picked it up.

She swung around and, in a bold gesture, swept the board over her head, the pain unbearable. She smiled, and the crowd roared. She knew they would. Her fingers trembled, her body refusing to keep up the charade. She lowered her arms, then turned and limped away.

A judge hurried over to her, his baggy shorts flapping in the breeze. "Do you want to make another run?"

The audience applauded, whistled, and stomped their feet, encouraging her to continue, but she shook her head, indicating her decision; she didn't have the heart to try again.

"No, thanks," she muttered, gazing up at the stands. She had something more pressing on her mind. She slipped into the crowd. Kids patted her shoulder and back and grabbed her hand, admiring her courage. She smiled broadly, but each touch hurt her.

When she was on the outside edge of the crowd, near the fence where asphalt met dust and dirt, she rested her board against her leg, held her hands above her eyes, shielding the blazing sunlight, and studied the bleachers. Had Justin and Mason really come back?

She wasn't sure she had seen them. She had been zipping at top speed, and the sun had been harsh, flashing in her eyes, but if they were here in Los Angeles, then that could explain her urge to run. She didn't see them now, but her moon amulet pulsed hot against her skin under her clothes.

Then she caught Catty, Vanessa, and Serena waving frantically at her. Did they want her to join them, or were they signaling something else? She picked up her board and started to push through the spectators toward them when someone grabbed her shoulder.

CHAPTER TWELVE

TIANNA TURNED, EXPECTING to find young kids bunched around her asking for her autograph. Instead, Justin and Mason towered over her, squinting against the sun. Unthinking panic rushed through her. She stepped back, her heart beating fiercely, and swung her skateboard in frantic sweeps to keep them away.

Their hands shot up, deflecting her blows, but they didn't try to nab her as she had expected. They stumbled off the asphalt against the wire-mesh fence and stayed there, watching her, waiting to see what she would do next. They looked as if they had been living on the street. Their T-shirts were soiled, jeans frayed, hair uncut and hanging in greasy clumps. A sour smell clung to them.

Music blasted and another skater broke loose, wheels jamming the concrete. The crowd roared, their feet stomping the bleachers in time to the beat.

Mason was saying something, but his words were lost in the thundering noise. He had shaved his goatee and his hair had grown back to its natural brown. The swagger had left his posture; his shoulders slumped and he clasped his hands together in supplication. What was he saying?

Tianna snapped off her helmet and let it fall by her feet. She strained to hear what he said. Past experience told her not to look into his eyes, but after one glance, she knew he no longer had the power to hypnotize her with his gaze.

She stepped forward, certain this was one more trick, but she had the weirdest feeling Justin and Mason were afraid of her now. Heat waves rose between them, the hot air releasing the tar and oil smells from the black pavement.

Sunshine glinted off the lens of Justin's glasses. He held his hand up to block the glare. A vicious scar now covered his arm where a standing goat had once been tattooed. "We want to apologize," he said at last.

She tilted her head, confused. She must have misunderstood; they couldn't be apologizing. She set her board between her knees, watchful, and grasped her moon amulet. It rested still and cold in her palm. It wasn't warning her of danger, but she let her power build anyway.

"We didn't come here to do anything more than say we're sorry!" Mason yelled, as if he sensed her energy growing. The green snake tattoo still curled on his neck, but now a scar just like Justin's slashed his arm as if a savage beast had ripped the goat tattoo from his flesh.

"Apologize for what?" she asked, sudden emotions stirring inside her. She remembered the night they had broken into her house when she was only a child. Were they trying to say they were sorry for killing her parents and her sister, Jamie? They had tormented her most of her life, keeping her on the run, forcing her to be always vigilant and to live in terror of being caught. Did they think they could erase all that with words?

"You have to understand," Justin said. "We'd never have done what we did if we'd known the truth. We didn't understand that by going into the past to fix things, we'd actually make a future the Atrox didn't want."

"Are you telling me it was a mistake?" Bitter grief and rage swept through her and her telekinetic power started to explode. She bundled it tightly inside her, but the keyed-up energy trembled and grew, becoming stronger than her ability to hold it back. The tips of her fingers jittered and she stared at Mason's scar, trying to regain her concentration.

He caught her examining his arm. He rubbed it gingerly, as if the mark still pained him. "The Atrox tore our tattoos off when we failed it."

"We're outcasts now because we were too eager, but we thought we were doing right," Justin said, and remorse crossed his face, as if he missed being a Follower.

"You became outcasts because I rescued the Daughters?" she asked, not bothering to hide her distrust. Outcasts were Followers who had failed in their attempt to please the Atrox. They were ostracized and no longer part of the world of either light or dark, but Justin and Mason had come close to destroying the Daughters. She didn't think the Atrox would have punished them for that. If anything, it would have urged them to try again.

Justin slouched toward her, hesitant, and gave her a dubious look. "You could make it right."

"Me?" She glared at them, positive their cowering was only the prelude to a brutal assault. "What do you expect me to do?"

"You could tell the Atrox we only meant to please it when we went into the past." Justin pushed his glasses back up on his nose in a nervous gesture.

"I thought the Atrox sent you." She stared at them. Maggie had definitely told her the Atrox had given them the mission to go back in time, so why were they lying to her about it now?

"We did it on our own," Justin explained. "We didn't know."

"Know what?" Tianna felt baffled now. Could Maggie have been wrong?

"We just didn't know what you were then," Justin said and raised his eyebrows as if he were trying to look sincere.

"You didn't know I was a Daughter . . . or going to be one?" she asked, wondering why that mattered.

Justin spoke, his eyes lowered. "We didn't know you were the *becoming.*"

A chill swept through her. *"Becoming?"* Tianna studied them, trying to understand what they were saying. Could this be what Stanton had meant when he'd said that all Followers were talking about her?

"Becoming what?" she asked.

Abruptly, the music stopped and the crowd applauded, then everyone crushed forward as the competition ended and the sponsors started the product toss. T-shirts and Frisbees flew into the air.

"I told you we shouldn't talk to her," Mason mumbled to Justin. "She doesn't know, and now we're probably going to be in more trouble than before."

"How can she not know?" Justin argued, but he was stepping away, his eyes filled with terror. "She's lying. She's got to be aware."

"Aware of what?" Tianna asked, frustrated, and marched toward them.

They turned, clumsily bumping against each other, and hurried away, casting backward glances over their shoulders, as if they didn't trust her. Irritated, she let her power loose. It exploded into whirling wind and shoved them harmlessly, flapping their T-shirts and spiraling dirt into a dust devil around them.

Vanessa, Serena, and Catty jostled through the crowd and joined her as the windstorm settled.

"We tried to get here as soon as we saw Justin and Mason," Vanessa explained. "Didn't you see us waving at you?"

"I did, but I didn't understand," Tianna answered, still studying Mason and Justin. They had slowed their pace and were watching her warily now.

"I tried to shoot you a mental message to warn you that they were standing behind you," Serena said. "But it's always been hard to reach your mind."

"Thanks for trying," Tianna said sadly. She let out a long sigh and carefully took off her elbow pads. The bruise on her arm had swollen, and it throbbed painfully now. Her fingers looked like blue sausages, but the bleeding had stopped.

"It was so scary seeing Justin and Mason again." Vanessa lifted her sunglasses.

"Were they threatening you?" Catty asked.

"No." Tianna shook her head, still mystified. "They wanted to apologize."

"Apologize?" Serena scowled. "For chasing you all those years, or for—"

"For both," Tianna interrupted.

"But why would they say they're sorry now?" Vanessa asked.

"They're outcasts, and they thought I could do something about it," Tianna explained.

"They wanted me to talk to the Atrox for them."

"As if." Catty laughed, then stopped abruptly and took off her cap. "You're serious. They really expected you to talk to the Atrox on their behalf?"

"That's what they said." Tianna shrugged. "I think they believed I could make the Atrox accept them back."

Vanessa slipped her hands into the pockets of her denim miniskirt and paused to consider the situation. "Why would they come to you? You hate the Atrox more than anyone. It has to be a trick. Maybe they're trying to get you to use your power or something."

"That's what I thought, too," Tianna said. "But I'm positive they're outcasts. The Atrox tore the goat tattoos from their arms. It looked like it had reached down to the bone and pulled out some muscle, too."

"Gross!" Catty rubbed her skin. "That's vicious. Did they become outcasts because you saved me?"

"She saved all of us," Serena put in. But then

she added, "I thought the Atrox favored them. Didn't it send them back into the past?"

"They said they went on their own without the Atrox knowing." Tianna watched Mason and Justin. They stood on the corner still looking at her. She wondered if they were going to try to talk to her again.

"Maggie said the Atrox had sent them." Vanessa took off her cap and ran her fingers through her thick blond hair. "She wouldn't have lied to us. Check it out, Serena. See if you can get inside their minds."

Serena lifted her sunglasses. Her eyes widened and her pupils dilated. She stood motionless, as if in a trance, her body tense, sending out thought waves. After a moment she made a face, as if she had eaten something sour. "They're not only outcasts, they're disgusting and vile. I didn't find anything but garbage thoughts. I could have gone deeper, but no way."

"They must be setting a trap." Vanessa nervously twisted her hoop earring.

"They said they didn't know I was the

becoming," Tianna added reluctantly, not sure why she felt hesitant to share this.

"What are you *becoming?*" Catty asked.

"They didn't say," Tianna answered and wondered if this were the reason Stanton had told her to be more cautious.

Serena scowled and shot Tianna an odd look. "Did you see Stanton recently?" she asked, accusation in her voice.

Tianna shook her head too quickly. She hadn't been aware that Serena had glided into her thoughts. She did her best to keep the memory of Stanton's visit hidden, but she sensed Serena prowling around the edges of her memories of that night.

"I think we'd better visit Jimena." Serena smiled and looked satisfied, as if she had finally found what she had been looking for. "We need to find out what the *becoming* means. Stanton warned me to be more careful now that the Atrox is stronger but I guess I'm not the only one he's been warning." She looked at Tianna knowingly, but didn't seem upset. "Did Stanton really think he could keep his visit with you a secret? I mean, why would he even try?"

Tianna shrugged. "Sorry."

"I don't like this," Serena went on. "Stanton's keeping something from me, and I can tell he's worried."

"What could be big enough to make him worry?" Vanessa asked, pulling out her car keys. "He's got more power than practically any-one."

Catty shook her head. "Let's go talk to Jimena. Those guys were big trouble for us before."

"I have my car." Vanessa started forward. "Come on."

Catty picked up Tianna's skateboard and car-ried it for her. They walked together toward the parking lot. "I'm starting to get creeped out about everything that's going on," Catty confessed, her red flip-flops snapping against her heels.

"Starting to?" Tianna held her helmet and pads. "How'd you like to have someone tell you you're *becoming*? It sounds like I'm going to turn into a pod person or something worse, like a werewolf." Tianna tried to joke about it, but fear curled tight inside her, making itself at home. What was she *becoming*?

CHAPTER THIRTEEN

VANESSA DROVE HER red '65 Ford Mustang down Pacific Coast Highway. Tianna and Serena rode in the backseat, smearing suntan oil on their arms and legs. The top was down and their hair tangled in the flow of air. They passed the tube of tanning lotion to Catty in the front, then sang the songs blasting from the radio and danced with their hands, shoulders moving with the beat. Guys in passing cars honked and shouted compliments.

Tianna loved the briny smell of ocean, the sunbeams glinting off the waves, and the feel of the car speeding past the crowded sands of Santa Monica State Beach. She could ride this way for hours.

Catty sprayed lightener into her hair. The lemon fragrance spun around them before the wind swept it away. She leaned over the seat and handed the bottle to Tianna. "Try it."

"Is that how you get your highlights?" Tianna asked, feeling as if life had returned to normal again. She didn't want the day to ever end. She squirted a few drops into her hair and rubbed it into the strands, then handed it to Serena.

After a few more miles, Serena leaned forward and tapped Vanessa's shoulder. "Slow down. Collin likes to surf around here."

Tianna lifted her sunglasses and gazed out at the sparkling water, then pointed across the street. "There's his utility van."

Vanessa did a quick U-turn. Tires screeched, and drivers in the opposing lanes slammed to a stop. Tianna clutched the door, ready to shoot her power out and stop the Jeep careening toward them. It zigzagged, then swerved again at the last moment, narrowly missing the Mustang. A cacophony of honks exploded around them. Vanessa waved as if the drivers were only saying hello, then turned the steering wheel with another sharp jerk and took a parking space. She hit the brake, and the car stopped with a jolt, inches from the bumper of a yellow Jaguar. Tianna lunged forward, then back.

"Woo-hoo!" Vanessa shouted.

"You have got to get some driving lessons," Catty said, still clutching the dashboard. "You almost got us smashed."

"They stopped for us." Vanessa smiled and plucked her keys from the ignition. She opened the glove compartment and pulled out a pair of binoculars, then opened the car door. "Let's go."

Tianna shook her head, still shaking from the near-collision, and slowly crawled from the car.

Serena joined Tianna at the edge of a sloping hill and pointed to a silhouette of a surfer shooting a wave. "That's got to be Collin."

Girls in wetsuits stood on the beach at the breakwater, hands shielding their eyes against the brilliant sunshine, and watched the lone surfer.

"I can't make out anyone in the water," Catty said. "How can you tell it's him?"

"Collin loves to show off." Serena started tromping over the ice plant down to the sand. "He always draws a crowd."

"You'd better look again." Vanessa caught up to Serena and handed her the binoculars.

Catty grabbed them first and stared into the lens. "Cool."

"What?" Serena took the binoculars from her. After looking, she added, "I don't believe it."

Then it was Tianna's turn. She looked out to sea. Collin straddled his board, bobbing in the water. Jimena was the surfer everyone was watching.

"She's totally awesome," Tianna said, admiring her style.

"When did Jimena become such a surf rat?" Catty asked.

"Collin has been teaching her," Serena explained. "But I can't believe how good she is."

As they neared the water's edge, the roar of surf drowned the traffic sounds from the highway, and winter-white seagulls with dark gray wings circled overhead, their squealing cries shrill and loud.

Jimena maneuvered the surfboard and popped it from the wave, shooting over the surface of the ocean before slamming back into the water. She straddled the board, then saw her friends, waved, and road the sudsy surf to shore. When she reached the shallow water, she jumped off, undid the Velcro cuff of the surf leash and carried the board under her arm. She looked incredible in her bikini, with its plunging neck and strings tied high on her hips. A smear of zinc oxide covered her nose and lower lip.

"Justin and Mason are back," Tianna said as soon as Jimena reached them.

"They're outcasts now," Serena added.

Jimena frowned and set her board on the sand. She drew back her hair and squeezed out the water. "Why are they outcasts?"

"We don't know why exactly," Catty put

in. "But they wanted Tianna to help them."

Jimena stared at Tianna, and the snakes on Jimena's Medusa stone came to life, their heads curling up as if to examine her.

"They told Tianna she was the *becoming*," Vanessa added.

"*¿Es cierto?*" Jimena looked surprised. "Are you sure you understood correctly?"

Tianna nodded, but her stomach tightened, remembering the way the word had made a chill rush through her, as if her body had recognized some danger in it.

Jimena pinched the Medusa stone between her fingers.

"Why don't you wear a moon amulet?" Vanessa asked peevishly. Something about Jimena had upset her. "Those snakes give me the willies."

Jimena smiled mysteriously. "Maybe I am wearing a moon amulet. The ancient Orphic priests called the moon the Gorgon's Head. Besides, this stone has the power to paralyze and terrify an enemy, and it guards against enchantment."

The snakes twisted and squirmed. Then Tianna blinked and the stone was an ordinary cameo again.

Finally, Jimena spoke, "Maybe Tianna is the *becoming*."

"What does that mean?" Tianna asked.

"I don't remember completely," Jimena said. "In the beginning of the ancient world, when Selene stopped the Atrox from destroying hope, the Atrox vowed to bring an unimaginable curse upon the world. Followers call it the *becoming*. The gods call it the *becoming sorrows*, but what that means I don't know yet."

"Do you think Tianna will do something?" Serena asked. "Maybe like Pandora, she'll release—"

"I would never do anything to hurt people." Tianna interrupted, folding her arms tightly across her chest. "Do you think I'd free disease and misery like Pandora? I'm not that stupid."

Catty put an arm around Tianna. "You'd never do it on purpose, but maybe—"

She shrugged off Catty's hand. "I wouldn't do it even by accident. Think about it. If the Atrox asked you to open a jar or a trunk, would you?"

Catty shrugged.

"But suppose there's something you're going to do or have already done that will start an unstoppable series of events," Serena suggested. "Like when you used the Secret Scroll—"

"Would you get off it?" Tianna shot back angrily. "I thought I could defeat the Atrox then."

Serena ignored her and looked at Jimena. "Do you think that could be it? Could Tianna have done something when she summoned the Atrox? Maybe the *becoming sorrows* only refers to a new era when the Atrox is stronger and Tianna would be the *becoming* because she helped it escape its binding."

"It's possible," Jimena agreed.

"She didn't do it intentionally," Catty added as if trying to protect Tianna from their accusations.

"Of course it was accidental," Jimena agreed, but there was doubt in her eyes. "Tianna would never do anything like that on purpose. We'll have to wait and see what happens."

"You don't seem to know much for an all-seeing goddess." Vanessa didn't bother to hide her frustration. "Do you think you could try a little harder to get your memories back? I mean, you're down here surfing, and we don't even know why you've come down to earth yet."

"I should have my memories back by now," Jimena responded, unruffled. "But staying at home isn't going to make them return faster. Maybe I'm destined never to remember. That's always a possibility. It's happened before."

"Never?" Serena whispered in a hopeless tone.

"You shouldn't come down to the beach with Collin like it's just an ordinary day," Vanessa said, her anger spilling out. "Maggie never would have. I wish she were still around."

"She won't be coming back," Jimena answered softly. "And I understand your frustration. You're angry with Maggie for abandoning you when you needed her most, and now you're redirecting your rage at me because you can't tell Maggie how upset you are with her for deserting you. But no matter what you do or how angry you get with me, it's not going to bring Maggie back, and it won't make me remember any faster."

"This sucks," Serena said suddenly, tears brimming in her eyes. "Stanton tells me the Atrox is stronger now, and we're more vulnerable, but he won't tell me why."

"When evil forces in the world become too strong, the Good in the universe always sends someone to restore harmony," Jimena said, her eyes piercing. "That doesn't mean we always win. This might only be the first battle."

Tianna caught something in Jimena's expression and suddenly the sun felt too hot, its glare too white and blinding. She clasped Catty's arm, feeling dizzy and nauseated. She was convinced Jimena knew more than she was saying. But why would she hold back? Tianna had the distinct impression that Jimena had returned to earth to stop her from *becoming*, but what did that mean?

CHAPTER FOURTEEN

TIANNA OPENED THE front door and stepped inside her home. The sound of television voices came from the living room, and the comforting smell of fresh-baked cookies warmed the air. She set her backpack, pads, and helmet down, then pulled on her sweatshirt. She didn't want Mary to see the bruises on her arm. Sunburn prickled her skin. She had less than an hour before Derek was picking her up for Jessica's party.

She had spent the day with Jimena, Catty, Vanessa, and Serena on the beach, trying to figure out what Justin and Mason had meant, but their conversation had only led them into frustrating circles, each idea winding back to the same conclusion: Justin and Mason had to be part of a larger scheme, but what?

Serena had left, promising to make Stanton tell her what he knew, but Tianna suspected Stanton wasn't going to let her know everything this time. She wondered if his hesitation had to do with the sword Maggie had used centuries back to bind the Atrox to its shadow. But she couldn't think about that now. She had to worry about Mary.

"Hi." Tianna stepped around the stone fireplace and walked to the corner of the room.

Shannon lay snuggled in a nest of pillows on the couch watching TV, but when she saw Tianna, she pressed the MUTE button on the remote and glanced behind her.

"What's wrong?" Tianna asked, sensing her fear.

Shannon leaned forward. "Todd needs to see you," she rasped in an odd whisper. "It's important."

Tianna plopped on the couch beside her and kicked off her shoes. Sand scratched between her toes. "Why are you whispering?"

Before Shannon could answer, Mary pushed through the swinging door from the kitchen, carrying a tray of chocolate chip cookies and milk. She wore a pant suit with a red shawl draped over her shoulder. "There you are. I was starting to worry about you."

Shannon pinched Tianna's wrist as if to silence her.

"I'm sorry I'm late," Tianna said. "We went down to the beach and time slipped away." She glanced back at Shannon. What had happened? Then a sudden thought shot through her. Could Todd's condition have become more critical?

"Your nose is sunburned." Mary interrupted her thoughts and handed her a glass of milk. "I have some ointment upstairs."

Mary sat on the arm of the couch and ran her fingers through Shannon's hair. Shannon pulled away and stared glassy-eyed at the TV, as if she were alone in the room.

"Show Tianna what you bought at the garage sale today," Mary coaxed.

Shannon picked up a brightly painted statue of a potbellied man with an elephant's head. "I bought a statue of Ganesha," she said, her eyes carefully avoiding Mary's. "He's the Hindu god of wisdom and good fortune and has the power to get rid of obstacles."

Mary smiled as if she were pleased with Shannon's response. "After we visited Todd, we stopped at garage sales all the way home. It was fun to see him, wasn't it?"

Shannon nodded, but she seemed depressed; something had stolen her normal rush of excitement. Maybe she wasn't feeling well.

"How is Todd?" Tianna picked up a cookie and immediately realized her mistake. She groaned.

Mary lunged forward and clasped her swollen fingers, turning her hand. She examined the scabs and black-purple bruises; then, with a nurse's skill, she rolled up Tianna's shirtsleeve and stared down at the knots of discoloration on her elbow and arm.

"You entered the competition after I told you not to." Her face folded into a fierce scowl. "I warned you it was dangerous."

"I was already signed up," Tianna started to explain. She felt bad that she had lost Mary's trust, but she didn't understand why Mary had been so restrictive. "I wore my helmet and pads."

"It's a good thing you did or you'd be in the hospital right now." Mary's chest moved up and down in hurried breaths, her anger obvious. "You have to learn that there are consequences to your behavior. I know you want to go to the party tonight, but you're staying home."

"I have to go. You don't understand," Tianna pleaded. "If I don't show up tonight, these two girls, Jessica and Corrine, will think they've gotten to me, and they'll only torment me more."

"You should have thought about that before you disobeyed me." Mary sounded completely unbending.

"Put me on restriction for a month," Tianna

said, trying to bargain. "I don't care for how long, just let me go out tonight."

"I've made my decision." Mary cocked her head, jaws clenched.

Something snapped and Tianna unleashed her anger. "It was wrong to tell me I couldn't compete after telling me I could. You knew how much I was looking forward to it."

"I don't appreciate your arguing with me when you know I'm right," Mary answered, her voice low, fierce, and calm. "Look at your arm and fingers. We need to get X-rays."

"I'm not going to the hospital!" Tianna yelled crossly, and rushed from the room. She bounded up the long winding stairs, her bad temper burning its way up her throat.

"Tianna!" Mary's footsteps pounded on the steps behind her.

Tianna flew into her room and slammed the door, then recklessly used her power to fuse the latch bolt into the catch. A wisp of smoke curled into the air with a hot, metallic odor.

"Tianna!" Mary yelled and pounded on the

door. "You know I don't like you to use your . . . ability. It's too dangerous."

Tianna ignored her and flopped on the bed, resentment tightening her chest. She stared at the ceiling and let her telekinetic power free. Soon, cracks split across the plaster, the tiny fissures spreading into the corners. She concentrated, and the yellow lanterns exploded. Shreds of papers swirled around her like a swarm of golden moths.

She swung her hands up and fired her energy, expressing her rage. The light fixture exploded. Electricity sizzled, and blue sparks crackled. The fiery display only made her hungry for more. She wanted to destroy.

"Tianna!" Mary shouted in complete frustration.

With brazen disrespect, Tianna flung a wave of air. The wooden door cracked with a terrible boom. Chunks of plaster fell from the ceiling.

Mary was quiet now, and the sudden silence made Tianna uneasy. What had she done? "Are you all right?"

Tianna held her power in check. It prowled

near the surface, petulant and strong, a primitive urge needing expression. She grimaced. She had been a brat, indulging in a temper tantrum. Why was she acting this way?

Her powers had always been stronger than those of the other Daughters, and her unexplained gift hadn't come from Selene. Was she by some angry twist of fate going to "become" a Pandora and release something dreadful on the world? Maybe her destiny had always been to destroy. Her stomach turned. What would happen if the energy inside her became stronger than her ability to hold it back? She imagined herself on a rampage, destroying everything in her path like some Godzilla monster.

Sudden terror ripped through her and she needed Mary's comforting arms. She shot her energy out and with a sudden whack broke the soldered latch. The door swung open, and Tianna rushed into Mary's arms.

"I'm sorry." Her shoulders slumped and she broke into sobs. "I don't know why I was acting that way."

Mary patted her back, soothing her. "It's hard being your age, but I've taken care of enough teens to know it's normal to get upset once in a while. It's just that most girls your age don't have a power to throw around. That's all."

Tianna sniffled and wiped her eyes.

"Next time we'll talk out our differences so we can each see both sides." Mary pulled back and looked at her with loving tenderness. "We'll put the past behind us. Rest tonight, and tomorrow we'll start a new day. We'll visit Todd. You always like to tease him."

Tianna nodded, but an odd feeling was growing inside her, and she knew she couldn't stay at home. She had to party. No way was she going to miss out. She might not like Jessica, but everyone talked about her house in the Hollywood Hills, and Tianna wanted to see it. Besides, Michael's band was going to play, and she needed to see Derek. But mostly she wanted to dance. It always made her forget her misery.

Mary continued making plans for their outing tomorrow, but Tianna pulled away, resolute with a plan of her own. "I think I'll take a shower and go to bed early."

"That's a good idea," Mary said. "You'll feel better tomorrow. You'll see."

Tianna nodded and closed the bathroom door. She turned on the shower and stripped, shedding sand on the rug. She felt jittery, but not from anger now. She was nervous because she was going to sneak out of the house.

For no reason that she could understand she thought about the e-mail Corrine had sent to Derek, pretending it was from Tianna. She wondered what it had said. She slid her hands through her hair and her imagination ran away with her.

Maybe it was time to tell Derek yes after all. A pleasant ache rushed through her, and she stepped into the shower, steam rising around her, her body ready. She had had enough daydreams about doing it. Derek had been her first kiss. Why not let him be her first lover?

CHAPTER FIFTEEN

AFTER HER SHOWER, Tianna pulled on her robe and went downstairs. Mary and Shannon sat curled together on the couch, watching a video and eating popcorn, even though the plate of cookies was still full.

"I'm going to bed," Tianna lied and stuck her hand in the bowl. Butter covered her fingers. She popped a salty kernel into her mouth and wondered if Mary's vitamins and nutrition drinks were her way of compensating for their diet of junk food.

"Good night, dear." Mary looked at her with such love Tianna almost changed her mind about sneaking out. Almost. She couldn't get Derek out of her thoughts.

Shannon leaned back, stretching into a yawn, an obvious ruse to hide her face from Mary. *Todd,* she mouthed, her eyes pleading. *Go see Todd.*

At least, those were the words Tianna thought Shannon was forming. But why was it so important for her to visit Todd without Mary's knowing? She nodded, making a mental note to see Todd in the morning.

She rushed back up the stairs to her room, closed the rickety door, and threw off her robe. She pulled on her silver miniskirt, loving the way it showed off her hip bones and belly ring, then she twisted into a black cropped top. The sleeves covered her arms from wrist to shoulder and hid the worst of her bruises. She stretched and let the neckline slip low.

Her heart raced with anticipation. She took a deep breath, trying to quell her excitement about telling Derek her decision. Then she stared into the mirror, brushed on glitter eye shadow, and added sparkle to her hair. Tiny diamonds glimmered against her black curls. She pasted three pink stars on her cheek, then squeezed strobe cream into her palms and rubbed it over her legs. Her skin glowed, and the sweet fragrance of gardenias scented the air. She angled one foot in front of the other and cast a sly smile at her reflection. A thrill rushed through her. She looked like an enchantress.

She opened her bedroom window and let the wind rush in. It skimmed over her with a gentle caress, awakening a mysterious force inside her, and for a moment she had the oddest feeling that if she had leaped back, the breeze would have carried her to the yard below.

Instead she used her telekinetic power to push out the screen. It hovered in the air outside. She willed a nearby branch to move closer to the sill. The old tree creaked and groaned, bending to her command, its leaves twitching toward her.

When the thick limb stopped in front of her, she stepped barefoot onto the rough bark, holding her high-heeled sandals in one hand. Then, like a tightrope walker, arms swinging for balance, she crossed the branch to the trunk, her toe rings catching the street light.

She turned and with a glance snapped the screen back into the window frame, then clambered down and jumped onto the soft grass. The branches whipped back into place, murmuring with song. A few leaves burst free and whispered around her. She smoothed out her skirt, brushed off her feet, and slipped into her shoes, tying the straps around her ankles.

Headlights flashed over her.

At first she didn't recognize Derek's car, because the engine whirred so easily, but the dented front bumper was unmistakable; duct tape kept it strapped to the front grille.

She strolled down the sidewalk to meet him, shoulders back and muscles tight, like a panther stalking its prey.

He pulled the car to the curb.

She opened the door and slipped inside, stretching her legs, willing him to look at her. His eyes met hers, but instead of a dreamy smile, she glimpsed something unexpected in his deep blue eyes. Was he angry with her?

"Mary told me I couldn't go to the party tonight, but I sneaked out to be with you." She gave him a silken smile, then kissed his cheek and breathed in his spicy scent. "I've made up my mind."

"About what?" He looked glum.

"About us?" She ran her fingers down his thigh to his knee, surprising herself with her bold touch, but he didn't seem to notice her provocative tease.

"What about us?" he asked, color flaring in his cheeks. He always turned crimson when angered. "Maybe there's something you should tell me."

"What do you mean?" She eased back and snapped the seatbelt around her, her spell-weaving mood gone.

He jerked the steering wheel, and the car pulled away with a jolt. He drove in silence all the way to Sixth Street, tension building between the two of them, and then he made a right turn and headed for La Brea, his fingers tapping on the steering wheel.

"I can't believe you'd do this to me, Tianna," he said, not bothering to hide his anger.

"Do what?" She tried to imagine what was wrong. She hadn't seen him since the previous night or even talked to him on the phone. Had he tried to call her? She hadn't checked her messages.

"I opened up to you. I told you how much I cared for you." He eased onto La Brea, heading north.

"I told you how much I liked you, too," Tianna answered and waited, breathless, for him to continue, her heartbeat frantic.

At the corner of Hollywood and Vine, showy neon lights streaked across the car hood in a flamboyant parade of colors.

"You should have told me, Tianna." His words came out at last. "It hurts more to hear about it from someone else."

"I don't know what you're talking about." She leaned in front of him, trying to glimpse his eyes;

then, frustrated, she used her power to stop the car in the intersection. "Seriously, I don't. Look at me, and you'll see I'm telling the truth."

Horns blared. Car after car sped around them, headlights sweeping over the rearview mirror reflected in Derek's stormy eyes.

"You've been seeing another guy." He stomped on the gas pedal, gunning the engine, trying to free the car from her telekinetic hold.

"There's no other guy," she protested.

"You're making a traffic jam!" he shouted in a burst of temper. "Release the car!"

"Not until you tell me where you got such a stupid idea," she said, her power raging inside her and wanting to do more than simply stop the car.

"I hate the way you're pretending like you don't know." He shot her a look. "You were just waiting for the right time to let me down so you wouldn't hurt my feelings. Did you think finding out this way wouldn't make me feel like a loser?"

She let the car go. The wheels skidded forward, and black clouds of burned rubber trailed behind them, the acrid stench filling the air.

Derek eased up on the gas and after another block turned the corner, heading away from the city lights.

"At least tell me who this other guy is." She stared out the window, wishing she had stayed home with popcorn and videos.

"Ethan."

"Great." She folded her arms over her chest, daring him to contradict her. "I don't even know anyone with that name."

"Right," he answered, scorn on his face.

He steered the car into a residential neighborhood. Soon trees and shrubs formed a tunnel, and darkness pressed around them. The streets became narrower as they climbed into the hills, the yards smaller, and then the lawns disappeared, and the sky again became visible overhead.

Derek parked against a sprawling white stucco house perched on the slope and turned off the engine.

The inimitable sound of Michael's band filled the night, but it did little to put Tianna back in a party mood.

"Look, either you believe me or you don't." She stared straight ahead. "If you cared for me the way you said, then you'd know I wouldn't do that to you. It's just not me. You see the way guys look at me. I see them stare. I know I can go out with them, but you're the one I like. I want to be with you."

She opened the car door and started up the hill, determined to party and dance and wipe away her miserable mood. Maybe she could get a ride home with Vanessa. If not, she'd borrow money from someone and take a cab.

Derek ran after her, his shoes pounding on the street. He put an arm around her and tentatively pulled her against him. "You're right. I'm pathetically jealous. Sometimes I look at you and wonder why you're wasting your time with me. I mean, I see the other guys who are after you."

She glanced down. An apology wasn't enough. "How could you not trust me?"

He kissed her temple. "Sorry," he whispered.

She sighed heavily, knowing it would be a long time before she could forget this.

Kids stood in the doorway, spilling out into the street, laughing and drinking sodas. Throbbing music wrapped around Tianna and Derek as they stepped inside. Derek grabbed her waist and started dancing, his eyes apologetic.

"I promise," he said over the pounding beat. "I'll never doubt you ever again."

But an odd sadness raced through her, as if somehow she sensed the lie in his words.

"You mean what you say right now," she said and tossed her head, trying to forget their argument and dance. "But you won't keep your promise."

"Come on. Let's go look at the moon." Derek took her hand and pulled her through the living room.

Gossamer white curtains billowed around the open sliding doors. Tianna and Derek stepped out onto the deck. The terrace stretched along the length of the house, overlooking Los Angeles. The moon added a fairy-tale glow to the cityscape.

"It's breathtaking," Tianna whispered.

But Derek wasn't looking at the view; he was glaring at someone in the crowd.

She turned.

Derek pointed. "That's Ethan. He's been bragging about being with you."

Tianna stared, surprised. It was the guy who had shot her the angry look in Planet Bang the night before. "I don't even know him."

Corrine danced with him, her hips brushing against his. She caught Tianna looking at her and waved as if they were still best friends. Then she grabbed Ethan's hand and started pushing through the dancers to join them.

"Why's she coming here?" Derek looked as if he wanted to escape.

"She wants to torment me." Tianna sighed.

Corrine wore a crisp white shirt. Only two buttons were fastened, and every swing of her hips revealed a triangle of flesh and the gold chains draped around her incredibly thin waist. But her style wasn't what had caught Tianna's attention. She wore a charm on a chain around her neck that matched the silver wolf pinned on Ethan's lapel.

Tianna remembered the wolves on her front

lawn, the sorrowful song of their yelping. Maybe it was only a coincidence, but an odd chill rushed through her.

"You like my pin?" Ethan's voice startled her and she gazed into his eyes, suddenly aware that Derek was watching her. Did she look too eager?

"It's nice." She clasped Derek's hand, but he pulled away. Then her fingers found her moon amulet. The charm felt fiery against her clammy palm.

She stepped back, feeling dizzy and faint, her back pressed painfully against the cold metal railing. She stared at Ethan, at his dark eyes and unruly hair. The face of the young man in her dream had been hidden beneath the rim of a fedora. Could that guy have been Ethan?

CHAPTER SIXTEEN

"**H**EY, TIANNA, DO you want to dance?" Ethan's tone was too familiar, his smile overconfident. He stared at her in a suggestive way, as if trying to make Derek jealous.

No wonder Derek had been so upset. Ethan creeped her out, too. His black clothes and flashy jewelry made him a spectacle, but she sensed he enjoyed the stares.

"I think we need to talk." She tilted her head, determined to tell Ethan off, but before she could start, he grabbed her hand.

Derek didn't stop him. He didn't even try.

"Sure." Ethan pulled her into the crush of dancers, his fingers uninvited, already stroking her bare hip. The chains on his wrists were icy cold and sent shivers up her back.

"I didn't want to dance." She shoved hard. Her finger snagged the wolf pin. The sharp metal sliced her skin. Anger and pain made her power roam dangerously close to the surface. She could feel it humming, eager to attack. She took deep breaths, trying to control herself, and glanced back, hoping to find Derek. Where had he gone?

Ethan shot her a brazen smile and winked. "I like girls who play hard to get."

"As if." Tianna strained to keep her tele-kinetic power harnessed, but it bucked wildly, trying to break free. She really hated this guy and wanted to send him crashing into a wall. Instead she bit her lip and sucked her energy in, remembering the damage she had done to her bedroom. She couldn't let that happen here.

"You'll be mine," Ethan said in an insolent whisper. His broad shoulders leaned closer, overbearing, pressing against her and making her feel too frail and small.

Corrine stepped between them. "You and I are the ones who need to talk," she said, and she pulled Tianna away, leading her through the throng of kids dancing on the terrace, back inside the house, and around the corner into the dining room, where Michael and his band played.

Vanessa waved when she saw them. She hit a tambourine against her hip, looking fantastic in her low-slung, flared pants, her attitude all vixen.

Jessica's younger sister and her friends stood nearby, apparently crushing on Michael and watching him play the guitar. His fingers ran over the frets, his concentration intense.

The drumbeat hammered through Tianna, and she grudgingly followed Corrine into the sultry kitchen. Wontons sizzled in a pan on the stove, and a woman mashed avocados for guacamole.

Corrine stopped near a counter. Chopped onions and peppers sat in glass bowls.

"What's with you?" she asked angrily. "Do you have to have Ethan, too?"

Tianna stared at her, the onion vapor burning her eyes. "What do you mean, *too?*"

"Like you don't know." Corrine slammed her hand down near a basket of tortilla chips on the sideboard. "First you take Derek away from me—"

"Derek?" The accusation startled Tianna, and she lost her concentration. Her energy swept out, toppling the basket and spilling the chips. "Is that what all this is about? You like Derek?"

"Don't act as if you didn't know." Corrine placed her hands on her waist, too angry to notice the falling chips. "I was totally in love with him, and you went after him anyway."

"You should have told me." Tianna stared at her, frustrated. "He would have been off limits if I'd known."

"Like that ever stopped you," Corrine answered, her bitterness obvious. "Girls are getting tired of the way you steal their guys away."

"I don't—"

"You do. Guys are obsessed with you because they know you want to score."

Tianna stared at her, exasperated. "Where did you get such a crazy idea?"

"It doesn't matter. You should have asked around before going after Derek."

"Who could I have asked?" Tianna said impatiently, her energy thrumming and slipping out. A breeze blew through the kitchen, ruffling paper plates and tipping cups over, but Tianna knew it was her telekinetic power, popping out on its own. She pulled it back and spoke. "You were my only friend my first week at school, and you never mentioned him."

"That's because you started flirting with him right away." Corrine seemed determined to defend her hatred, as if feeling a bad emotion were better than feeling none at all.

Tianna brought her arms across her chest and squinched her eyes, thwarting the raging force inside her. "So, to get even with me for something you thought I did on purpose, you've been spreading rumors to ruin my reputation?"

"You think I'm the only one bad-mouthing you?" Corrine smirked. "Lots of girls hate you."

"I don't need to hear any more of this trash." Tianna turned abruptly, but that wasn't the reason she wanted to leave. She bundled her energy inside her as best she could, but the effort made her body cramp. She was only seconds away from a catastrophe. She darted from the kitchen and raced back around the band, shoving through the dancers. The speaker toppled, and feedback screeched. Kids stopped dancing and grabbed their ears.

Tianna jammed her way into the crowd, frantically looking for Derek. Then, without warning, strong hands clasped her shoulders.

"No!" she shouted and fought down her telekinetic power, but it was stronger now.

She pitched forward in a graceless stumble, falling into Ethan.

He smiled and caught her. "I knew you'd come back," he teased, his hands intrusive, embracing her boldly.

But his unwanted touch only fed her energy. She jerked away, unable to control her arms and legs. What was her power doing to her now?

Kids gathered around her, staring. She tried to smile, to reassure them, but her lips stretched into a grimace. She lurched forward and, in a bungling attempt to stop herself, slammed each foot down hard; but the telekinetic force was stronger, and it rocked her back and forth, making her shift from side to side as if she were break dancing.

Catty and Serena pushed through the kids circling her.

What is it? Serena shot into her mind.

My power, she thought back. *It's out of control and making me do this.* She swooped down into splits, then glided up again into a stand. Kids thought she was showing off and applauded.

Serena whispered to Catty, but they didn't seem distressed. Catty smiled as if she thought Tianna's predicament were funny.

"Go, Tianna!" she yelled, circling her fisted hands in front of her and chanting the words with the beat.

Serena whooped and joined Catty, dancing like twins. "Great moves!"

Get me out of here! Tianna pushed the thought at Serena, but she didn't know if Serena had caught it; then she clenched her teeth as the invisible hands lifted her shoulders high and whirled her around in a breathtaking defeat of gravity. She had to get out of there before she seriously injured someone with a head butt or worse.

Kids clapped and whistled, yelled her name, and called for more.

"Woo-hoo!" Vanessa shouted, joining the rowdy mix.

Suddenly Derek plowed through the crowd.

"Help me!" Tianna shouted, and shot him a desperate look.

Without hesitation he grabbed her arm and wrenched her free of the unseen hands. Together they elbowed through the kids who had been pressing forward to watch her.

As soon as they were outside, she released what little hold she still had over her energy. It shot into the sky, speckling the night with glimmering flecks of light. Wind churned, and the red and blue embers sprinkled down to the street, leaving a fine residue of purple ash over Derek's car.

"I'm in control again," she whispered. She took several deep breaths, then touched his chest. "Do you want to go back to the party?"

He pulled away from her and opened his car door. "You go."

Her head shot up and she studied him. "What's up?"

"I saw the way you and Ethan looked at each other." He glowered. "I don't know if you've gone out with him or not, but it's obvious you want to hook up with him."

"I don't!"

"I can always tell when you're lying to me." Derek climbed in behind the steering wheel and slammed the door. "Your eye is twitching, Tianna."

"He annoys me," Tianna fought back and stepped closer. The expression on Derek's face scared her. "Don't say the words," she pleaded, knowing what he was thinking. "Please. Not now."

"Why keep it going, Tianna?" He spoke any-way and stuck his keys in the ignition.

Her heart sank. "I like you, and I know you still like me." She didn't want to hear what he was going to say next.

His face tightened. "I'll get over you, Tianna."

The words stunned her.

Derek started the car on the first try, the engine humming smoothly. Tianna grasped what she had missed before; he had used their trip money for the repairs. "How long have you been planning to break up with me?" she asked.

"It's not just Ethan. You and I both know it's been coming for a while. You've been distracted and distant when we've been together. It's proba-bly better if I just hang out with a regular girl."

"You love adventure," Tianna said. "You told me so."

"I changed my mind." He drove away.

She watched his car until it disappeared down the winding road. Her hurt tunneled deep inside her, nesting with her other sorrows. How many times was life going to hand her good-byes?

She didn't want to go back to the party, but she had to find someone to give her a ride home. She turned reluctantly and bumped into Ethan. How long had he been standing behind her?

"Were you listening?" she asked in disbelief.

"Derek is a real loser for breaking up with you," Ethan said, his smile enticing. "But it's good news for me. I've wanted to be with you for a long time."

"You don't even know me."

"I will," he said. His confidence irked her.

"Just leave me alone, okay?" She tried to walk around him, but he grabbed her arm and pulled her back.

"I always get the girl I want, Tianna, always," he said. "That's a promise."

"Not this time," she answered, with a promise of her own.

But that only made his smile broaden. "I'll catch you at school on Monday."

He walked down the street, his footsteps echoing behind him. He opened the door to a silver Corvette, but before he climbed in he shot her a look, his arrogant eyes inviting her to join him.

Tianna stood defiantly, her power throbbing with the desire to smash his car.

He climbed in and the engine roared, tailpipes growling. But instead of driving away, he backed up and stopped in front of her. The passenger-side window rolled down with a whir. He leaned over and looked up at her, his wheels inching forward impatiently.

"I love the chase, Tianna," he said. Then he released the brake and the car screeched off, leaving black tire marks on the street and thin smoke rising with the stench of burned rubber.

Tianna flung a heated bolt of energy. She didn't care if it was against the Daughters' rules. She wanted to wreck the Corvette. Her power dismantled a trash can, the pieces flying into the air and clattering to the ground, but the car was too fast for her. She took a sharp breath. What was she doing? She calmed herself, getting rid of her anger.

Laughter and the sound of running filled the night. She turned. Catty, Vanessa, and Serena ran down the street, looking gorgeous in slinky clothes, their legs long in high-heeled sandals, skin glowing.

"I thought you said it wasn't embarrassing when your powers messed up," Vanessa teased, her lips glossy. Tawny blush covered her cheekbones.

Tianna tried to laugh, but she wanted to sob. "Did I look that ridiculous?"

"It's okay, we love you anyway." Catty smiled sweetly. She wore silky short shorts and had drawn pink flowers and hearts down her right leg.

Then Serena touched Tianna's arm. "I wasn't snooping," she said apologetically. "But your thoughts are so strong they're slipping into the air. Why did Derek break up with you?"

"Derek broke up with you?" Vanessa sounded shocked.

Tianna shrugged. "I think the goddess bit got a little unnerving for him."

"Do you want me to take you back in time to fix it?" Catty asked, her eyes already dilating.

Tianna shook her head. "I wouldn't know which day to visit."

"He'll be back," Serena said with certainty. "I can read his thoughts so easily. He's totally crushing on you. Maybe he just got jealous tonight and was afraid he was losing you."

"Let's go back inside." Catty lifted her hands and playfully moved her hips against Tianna. "I'll dance with you if you promise not to do any of those crazy telekinetic moves."

Tianna smiled, but suddenly the need to see Todd overwhelmed her. "Thanks, but you guys stay. It's a great party. There's no reason for you to miss out."

"We won't leave you alone," Vanessa said, even though she obviously had to sing with Michael's band tonight.

"I'll be all right." Tianna looked at each one, grateful to have such good friends. "Besides, I want to visit Todd."

"I'll give you a ride," Vanessa offered.

Tianna shook her head. "I'll catch the bus."

Catty locked arms with her and started walking her down the hill toward the bus stop. "Derek's probably changed his mind already. He's so in love with you. Besides, you've got every guy at school crushing on you anyway."

"There's a lot more to life than having a guy," Serena added.

"That's weird, coming from you," Vanessa teased, but there was also accusation in her tone. "Considering we never see you anymore."

Serena smiled mysteriously. "Why do you always assume I'm with Stanton? Maybe I'm home practicing my cello and not answering the phone. Did you ever consider that my real passion is music?"

Tianna stared at her, wondering if that were true.

An hour later, Tianna had snuck inside Children's Hospital and was stealing past security guards and nurses' stations. She ran down a long corridor, carrying her sandals, her bare toes springing off the polished linoleum. The smells of medicine, oxygen, and antiseptic wafted around her.

At last, she peeked inside Todd's room. He lay on stark white sheets under a fluorescent light, monitors beeping beside him. His sunken eyes looked too old for a little boy. She had a peculiar sensation that he was fighting for more than his life. She winced, wondering where such an odd thought had come from.

She crept over to his bed and watched him sleep. His head lay at a stiff angle. When he didn't stir, she turned to leave. His small hand grabbed her wrist.

"Tianna," he rasped. His eyelids fluttered.

She lowered the guardrail and sat on his bed, careful of the needles in his arm and the plastic tubes connecting him to intravenous solutions dangling from stainless steel rods.

"I'm not going back to Mary's house," he said after a long swallow. "My caseworker thinks it's because I want to live in a home with boys."

"Is that what you wanted to tell me?" she asked.

"I needed to warn you." He tried to lift his head, but he slumped back on the pillow. "I got sick because I took your vitamins instead of mine."

She stared at him, surprised, but then she realized he was only trying to find an explanation for his sudden illness. Now more than ever she knew her unruly telekinesis had done something to him. "But I take those pills all the time, and they don't make me sick, so why would they make you ill?" she asked.

"Don't lie to me," he answered. "You always throw them away. Good thing. I think Mary is trying to poison you."

He started to fall back to sleep and she cuddled next to him, wishing she had the power to make him well. She stayed with him until she heard a cart rolling in the hall; a nurse had started making rounds to give out medicines. She climbed from his bed, kissed his forehead, then stole a blanket from the cabinet, wrapped it around her, and began the long walk home.

A few minutes later she was back on the street, strolling through a neighborhood of small bungalows. The homes were pressed together and overgrown with rosebushes, palms, and ferns. Shadows glided furtively across the lawns and darkness gathered around her, obliterating the silvery glow of the moon.

She had gone a short distance when her body tensed. She turned and caught a glimpse of movement under the dim streetlamp a block away. Someone had seen her turn back and had darted into the shadows beneath a jacaranda tree.

She didn't think it was only her imagination. She slowed her pace and listened. The hollow tap of footsteps filled the night. She considered using her power but hesitated. What if the person was only walking home as she was?

She grasped her amulet. It felt warm, but didn't glow yet. Maybe the danger was too distant still.

At the next corner, she hid behind a hedge and cautiously slipped out of her sandals, the concrete cold against her feet. She ran in silence across the lawn, the tail of the blanket flapping behind her, and took refuge in darkness under an overhanging bough.

She waited, listening, the intensity of her fear surprising her.

Dried leaves scattered under someone's hurried steps, closer to her now. The person paused, as if trying to find her again. Was it only coincidence, or was someone stalking her?

Instinct told her to crouch lower. She slipped beneath an oleander bush and peered out through the bobbing pink flowers. Wind rushed through the trees, shifting their shadows, and then she saw him, a black silhouette.

Without thinking, she dropped the blanket and lunged forward. She sprinted across the lawn and dove as he started to turn. She clutched his knees and tackled him.

He fell back and, in the same instant, vanished. Her arms grappled a breeze. She plummeted to the concrete and hit her head hard. She gasped, her body spread out on the sidewalk, numb and useless. Her amulet thrummed, alerting her to danger and urging her to stand, but she stayed still, her cheek against the grit and dust.

A phantom shadow moved closer, twisting beneath the streetlamp, and then fluttered over her.

CHAPTER SEVENTEEN

TIANNA REMAINED SPRAWLED on the sidewalk, desperately trying to call forth her energy. It lay dead inside her now, stunned. She struggled to sit up, but the pain was too great. A sibilant sound filled the air above her, and her skin prickled with static electricity. She squinted in concentration, her heart racing, and imagined herself blasting the Follower materializing over her.

Tianna waved her arm, but instead of discharging power, her fingers flushed with a reddish glow, and light radiated down the sidewalk, pulsing before it went out.

"Great," she groaned, furious with her telekinetic power for abandoning her at the moment when she needed it most.

"You're too reckless," a familiar voice said, the tone strong and deep.

She glanced up. "Are you controlling my power?"

"Of course I am." Stanton formed from black vapor, a devious smile on his face. "You need to think before you act. You could have hurt me."

"Then why were you following me like some stalker?" she snapped, wishing her head would stop hurting. "You scared me, you know? You could have just appeared and told me what you wanted. Or waited until I got home."

He knelt beside her, his hand brushing the loose hair from her face. "I wasn't the only one following you," he whispered. "Didn't you see the flash of black lightning?"

"No," she whimpered, rubbing her neck. She

wondered if the bolt were the same dazzling shard of darkness she and Madame Oskar had seen in the misty skies the night before. "I'm not worried about it. It's probably just a missile shooting off from Vandenberg Air Force Base. I'm more concerned that someone was following me."

He gave her a quizzical look. "I told you to be more cautious," he scolded. "You shouldn't be out late at night walking alone."

"I guess there are a lot of things I shouldn't do," she countered, trying to figure out what he wanted from her this time.

He helped her sit up, then stand, his hands comforting and sure. He took off his jacket and wrapped it around her, protecting her from the cold. His thoughtfulness surprised her, and she wondered if he treated Serena with the same tenderness. He pulled her gently into darker shadows beneath a trellis of night-blooming jasmine, the sweet fragrance flowing around them.

"Why would you want to protect me?" She stared at him, confident that was what he had been doing. She wished she had had Serena's ability to go into his mind and read his thoughts. She sensed his evil, but she also sensed something decent and good in him.

"I didn't say I was protecting you," he answered at last, his breath sweet and fresh. "I said I wasn't the only one following you."

She stared at him, her mind immediately turning to Ethan. "Who was the other person?"

He ignored her question and asked one of his own. "Hasn't Pandia—Jimena gotten her memories back yet?"

Tianna shrugged. "Jimena didn't go to the party tonight, because she was going to try self-hypnosis to see if that would work."

"She should know by now," he whispered, his eyes suddenly more cautious.

"Know what?" she said in the low voice, sensing his watchfulness. And then another thought came to her. Maybe his concern had something to do with the sword. If it was power-ful enough to bind the Atrox, then it must have potent magic. Perhaps he thought Jimena would know where to find it once she had retrieved all her memories. "Just tell me. Is it about the sword?"

His blue eyes softened, and a chill rushed through her head. He was reading her thoughts and stirring deep inside her memories. Did he think she knew where the sword was hidden?

Recollections unfolded and closed in a swirling rapidity that made her dizzy. Then something unbearably evil skipped across her consciousness. She flinched, shocked by what she saw, and tried to clasp the memory. Before she could catch it, the vision slipped back into oblivion, leaving her with nothing but a looming sense of doom.

"What was it?" she asked. "Tell me, please. What did I glimpse in that memory?"

"I'm not sure." He stared at her with unfathomable sadness. "I pulled up so many."

Her heart raced, knowing that he was lying to her. "What were you looking for in my mind?"

"I want to help you before you *become*," he said simply.

Panic and dread tore through her and she

began to tremble. "That's the same word Mason and Justin used." She started to ask him what it meant, but before she could, he placed a warm finger on her lips.

She followed his gaze. Brilliant bolts of blackness scraped across the sky. She blinked, as if she were looking at the sun.

"What is it?" she whispered harshly.

Stanton started to speak, but before he could, the raven shadow flashed with lightning speed, streaking into jagged ripples around scattered clouds. Power surged in the street lamps, then went out, plunging the neighborhood into darkness.

Ancient rhythms filled her chest, and her heart skipped a beat. She froze, sensing a vicious predator coming closer.

"It's the Atrox, isn't it?" she whispered, knowing that it was.

"Its power is unimaginable now." He pulled away from her and started to fade.

"Take me with you," she pleaded, terrified he'd refuse.

CHAPTER EIGHTEEN

SUDDENLY STANTON slammed against her. She shuddered and grasped her amulet. She had made a horrible mistake; she shouldn't have trusted him. They catapulted into the air and disintegrated.

The night throbbed through her with a fierce richness she had never imagined. Secret nocturnal songs came to her from crickets, rats, and toads, and in the same moment the luxurious smells of pine and eucalyptus trees became part of her, as did the surprisingly lush taste of churning fog and ocean mist.

She rustled through palm fronds after Stanton, no more than a gloomy apparition; then, without warning, she fell back into her body. Her feet hit solid ground, jarring her knees. She let out a foolish whimper, then blinked and licked the flavor of the night from her lips. She looked around, surprised to find herself standing near her front porch. She rubbed her chest, trying to coax her heart into a slower rhythm, then leaned against the iron railing, overcome with dizziness. She hoped she wouldn't vomit, right there in front of Stanton, but then she did.

"Most people get ill the first time they turn to shadow." Stanton stood beside her, holding back her hair while she threw up on the lawn. "And this trip was worse than normal. We had to leave quickly or be caught."

She wiped her face on her sleeve, then remembered she was wearing his jacket. "Sorry," she said.

"Keep the jacket," he answered with a smirk.

She nodded. Even though she sensed his evil, she felt she could trust him now. "Can you tell me what you were going to say?"

When he didn't answer, she glanced around. He had left without her even noticing.

Slowly she walked up the porch steps and summoned her power to unlock the front door. The dead bolt and latch slid back, and the door creaked open. She slipped quietly inside, not wanting to wake Mary. She carefully closed the door and listened. Soothing warmth gathered around her, and her tense muscles began to relax. The house was silent. She felt certain both Shannon and Mary were asleep in bed.

She started up the stairs, her body still aching from the fall. Much worse, this night had broken her determination. She had had enough. She wasn't going to stay. Living on the street had taught her to trust her intuition, and she had been foolish to ignore it for so long. Right now, being a goddess was downright scary, and Los Angeles was weird. She didn't know what Stanton was after, but she didn't care to stick around and find out. She decided to leave that night. Besides, by staying, she would only have been putting others in danger; she didn't know how long she could trust herself to keep her telekinetic energy contained.

Moonlight cast a milky glow across her room. She hurried to her closet, stripping off Stanton's jacket. She flung it on the bed, then slipped from her party clothes. She tossed her moon amulet on her dresser, but as she started to pull on her baggy jeans, she caught her reflection in the mirror and stopped.

A small red blister marked her chest where the amulet had rested against her skin. She stared at it, baffled. Was it only because she had been with Stanton or did it mean more? Each Daughter had a dark side, and when it became stronger than her will to hold it back, the amulet burned, scarring her skin.

As far as she was concerned, the festering mark was only one more reason to run. She yanked on her baggy sweatshirt, then sat on the edge of her bed and pulled on thick socks and boots. At last she grabbed her backpack and began stuffing deodorant, toothpaste, aspirin, and clothes inside. She wished she had saved more money.

"Tianna?"

She gasped, startled, and whipped around.

Mary stood at her door, in a pink bathrobe, her wig at an odd angle, one curl almost covering her right eye. "What's wrong, dear?"

"I'm leaving," Tianna whispered.

Mary stared at her for a moment. "Don't you like the home I've made for you?" In the dim light Mary looked as if life had drained from her.

"It's not you." Tianna felt guilty. How could she explain? "You've been great, but if I stay any longer I'd only be putting you, Shannon, and Todd in danger. There's something really creepy about my power. I'm scared of what I might do."

Mary stepped into the room. "You can't leave."

"I can, and I will." Tianna swung her backpack over her shoulder.

Mary tried to stop her with a hug, but Tianna pushed her way around her and started toward the stairs. She didn't dare look over her shoulder. She was too afraid that seeing Mary's kind face would weaken her resolve.

"You can't go," Mary called after her in a soft, haunting voice. "Because you're the *becoming*."

Tianna turned slowly, her heart hammering painfully inside her chest. The hallway seemed to spin around her. She glanced back.

Mary had walked across her room and now stood in the moonlight cascading through the window. Her eyes glowed phosphorescent yellow.

CHAPTER NINETEEN

"WHEN DID YOU become a Follower?" Tianna dropped her backpack and sank down on the edge of the bed, feeling defeated, weak, and powerless, the way she had felt the night her family had been killed. She winced, sure she was to blame for this as well; Mason and Justin had broken into Mary's home when she had first come to stay. "If Mason and Justin did this to you, maybe the Daughters can still free you."

"I was a Follower long before they were even

born." Mary gave her a frosty smile and flung off her wig. Her skull was tattooed in an elaborate green-and-blue design. "Do you like the way I've been using Todd and Shannon as a cover? Pretty clever, right? That's why the Atrox uses me for its most crucial assignments; I know how to blend in with civilians."

Tianna nodded dumbly, feeling light-headed, and thought of Stanton now. Had he known what Mary was all along? Maybe that was the reason he had told her to be more cautious.

Mary stepped back into the moonlight to close the blinds, and for the briefest moment the pale luminescence turned to silver fire, radiating over her tattoo with an otherworldly glow. Mary turned, her face resplendent and suddenly beautiful. She caught Tianna watching her and strutted toward her, her pride immense.

"Who would have thought I was a Follower, with my little goody-goody act? I even fooled Mason and Justin. They almost ruined everything, poking around. I couldn't believe the way they were going to sacrifice you, down at the ocean. Were they such fools that they didn't know? They deserve to be outcasts now."

Tianna blinked, struggling to get over her shock and to focus on a way to escape. She tried to concentrate, but her mind felt muddled. Did Mary have some kind of control over her after all?

"I'm so tired of this charade." Mary stretched sensually and her evil leaked out, seething around Tianna like a poisonous breath. Mary slipped out of her robe. Underneath, she wore a strange, misshapen snakeskin leotard. She stepped closer, as if she were putting herself on display.

Tianna took a deep breath and leaned back, feeling ill.

Mary swirled. Emerald-green and bloodred scales formed an intricate pattern running over her chest and shoulders, ending in spiny knots on her back, and now Tianna could clearly see that the tattoo was actually an astonishing layer of minute, overlapping plates, like those on the head of a snake.

"What are you?" Tianna had thought Mary had been brave and protective, but now she knew the reason Mary had been able to remain so calm when a year before Mason and Justin had threatened her. She was far more powerful than they had ever been. Tianna's chin trembled, and unexpected tears came to her eyes. Her reaction surprised her, but then she understood; she had so desperately wanted a mother that it had been easy for Mary to deceive her with her kindness act.

"Maggie told me you had lost your family," Tianna said, wondering why Maggie would have deceived her, too.

"Your beloved Maggie—that ancient hag— she's been my nemesis for years, but I fooled her this time," Mary bragged. "She believed everything I put into her mind."

"You tricked Maggie?" Tianna asked, wiping her eyes.

"She came blundering around, thinking I wouldn't feel her presence," Mary explained. "But of course I did. Someone with such powers as hers sends out vibrations as strong as a low-flying jet. So when I sensed her spying on me, I filled my mind with all these sad thoughts about my husband and children, lost to me forever in a bizarre flash flood in Ventura County. Boo-hoo. Maggie swallowed all my lies. I should get an Academy Award."

"It seems like a lot of bother," Tianna said.

The overconfident smile on Mary's face wavered.

"I mean, what did you gain from such a masquerade?" Tianna asked. "You worked yourself into a frenzy, and your room looks like hell"—at this Mary's eyes widened—"you spent all your time chauffeuring and sleeping in hospitals, for what? You have no life of your own."

"You don't know who you are. You really don't have a clue, do you?" Mary seemed both awed and surprised. "A pity for you, but, as for me, I serve the *becoming*."

"What is that?" Tianna asked petulantly, trying to stand. Her feet felt unsteady, and she wasn't sure she could take a step. She plopped back down again. "Why does everyone think I'm supposed to know?"

Mary laughed. "You would know if you'd taken your vitamins, but that's not my failure, it's yours." She folded her arms tightly over her chest. "It's going to be much harder on you now."

"Vitamins? You're still worried about those damn vitamins."

Mary glared at her. "For a goddess, you take a long time to figure things out."

"I'm not really a goddess," Tianna muttered. "If I were, my life wouldn't be such a wretched mess."

Mary started out the door. "Now, be a good little Daughter, and wait here for the Atrox."

"Right," Tianna said. The initial shock was wearing off, and she tossed Mary an audacious scowl. She picked up her backpack and on shaking legs made her way toward the door. She let her power grow until it sparkled around her in an endless flow, a halo of menacing righteousness. "I can't attack you, but I can defend myself," she threatened.

Mary didn't seem concerned. "Why would I want to harm you? Soon you'll welcome me as a sister."

Tianna bumped around her and walked into

the hallway. Mary did nothing to stop her, and that made her more nervous than if she had.

"But if you care for Shannon," Mary said sweetly. "You'll stay put. She'd make a nice little Follower, don't you think?"

Tianna turned back.

Mary raised one eyebrow. "The Atrox will come for you at the first glimmer of dawn."

CHAPTER TWENTY

TIANNA PACED, CLENCHING and un-clenching her hands. Angry sparks flared from the tips of her fingers. She hated feeling helpless. She stared at her bedroom door and loosened her power, letting it push forward. The wood bulged outward, then in, as if it were alive and breathing. She had less than three hours before dawn. No matter what the danger, she had to run. The longer she stayed, the greater her risk of *becoming*, what-ever that meant. She could easily escape on her own, but she couldn't leave Shannon behind.

She bit her lip, then made up her mind and slipped her moon amulet on. The white-hot metal scorched her skin, but she needed its warning now. She inched the door open, wondering why Mary had been so sure she wouldn't try to leave, and peered into the hall, her stomach sinking with fear.

The darkness writhed, then turned and fixed its attention on her. Were the billowing forms shape-shifters assigned to guard her door, or was the slithering movement only a phantom of her adrenaline-fueled brain?

She squinted, her muscles tensing. She couldn't stay poised indefinitely in the doorway expecting Mary and her guard-dog shadows to make the first move. She stepped tentatively forward, and immediately the demons descended upon her, thin narrow claws tracing through her hair. A scream rose from her lungs, but she clenched her jaw, choking it back, suddenly aware that it was her own energy crackling around her in jagged bolts of static electricity that had created the feeling of wicked talons scratching her scalp.

She drew her power back and held it tight, relief flooding through her.

Silence slipped around her again, and the strange shadows shifted away. She stood in front of Mary's door and released enough force to melt the latch. A tiny blue flash leaped into the air, and a white flame sealed the lock.

That done, she rushed down the hall, her telekinetic power murmuring around her and ruffling the air. A terrible fear grew inside her; maybe Mary had already turned Shannon into a Follower, and she was standing sentry somewhere in the house, eyes radiant, waiting to pounce.

The door was open, and a night-light shed an orange glow over the baseball bats in the corner. Tianna tiptoed into Shannon's bedroom and crossed soundlessly to her bed.

Shannon slept peacefully beneath posters of skateboarders, cuddling her pillow.

Tianna let out a long sigh and gently shook her shoulder. "Shannon," she whispered.

Shannon turned, her eyes heavy with sleep.

She glanced at Tianna's flaming moon amulet and sat up with a jolt, wide awake. "What is it?"

"We have to leave," Tianna said in hushed tones.

Shannon nodded calmly and climbed from bed, already reaching for the jeans flung over the chair near her nightstand. She pulled them on, not bothering to remove her green pajamas. Her reaction wasn't what Tianna had expected. Maybe a lifetime of medical emergencies had accustomed Shannon to being roused in the middle of the night.

"Be quiet," Tianna warned, worried that Shannon might start asking questions, but before she had finished speaking, a sharp winter cold cut through her, unwelcome and forbidding. Her body tensed, and she made her thoughts go blank, afraid even to draw a breath.

Now she understood why Mary had been so unconcerned about her escaping. She was still in Tianna's mind! She had never dropped her telepathic hold. It pinched tighter now, threads spreading out, examining Tianna's thoughts as if something had jarred it and made it quicken its hold.

"We have to leave now," Tianna urged, hating the squirming feeling in her head.

Shannon hurriedly zipped and buttoned her jeans, then yanked on a red sweater. She grabbed three brown pill bottles from her dresser, dropped them in a backpack, pulled the straps over her shoulders, and slipped into her shoes without uttering a sound. She walked quickly to her bedroom door, as if this odd emergency were routine for her. Tianna followed her.

At the top of the stairs, Tianna crouched and waited, holding her breath, straining to hear any sound that didn't belong. She rubbed her temples against the throbbing pressure inside her head and looked down at the entryway, searching the dark corners; anyone could be hiding there.

Tianna tried to tell herself that she had nothing to fear from Mary. She was positive her powers were stronger, but then she glanced at Shannon, so fragile, wide-eyed, and trusting, with her hair still tangled from sleep, and Tianna worried that she wouldn't be able to keep Shannon safe. Her anxiety spilled over and her heart began to pound as she realized Mary had finally discovered her plan to escape.

Immediately Mary awakened and screamed. Shannon stumbled backward, startled by the sound. Tianna caught her before she fell, then grabbed her hand and started down the stairs, but on the third step Tianna faltered, unsure. What might be waiting for them outside?

Mary pounded on her sealed door, shrieking with savage rage. Wood splintered, and the air filled with the primal vibration of hatred.

"Make her think we left," Shannon said, her face shining in the glow of Tianna's moon amulet.

Tianna understood and concentrated. Then, using her telekinetic power, she hit each step. The clatter of running footsteps rang through the house, and then, with a thought, she flung the front door open. It banged against the wall, fracturing its hinges. Shattered pieces of metal bounced across the tiles.

Together Tianna and Shannon ran back to

the hallway and hid behind the door to Todd's room. In her mind's eye, Tianna envisioned the front yard and street, hoping to deceive Mary and make her think they had left the house. She hoped her mental decoy would work.

Mary's door exploded outward, and Mary lurched from her bedroom, a wild grin on her face, her body misting out as she hurriedly changed into darkness and stretched past them, screaming in a torrent of wind.

"We need to go up in the attic," Shannon said.

Tianna stared at her, perplexed, wondering why Shannon didn't collapse into hysteria and scream.

Shannon answered her look. "She's a space alien. Did you just figure that out?" She didn't wait for an answer but led Tianna back to her room.

Moments later they stood in Shannon's walk-in closet, staring up at the trapdoor.

"How do you get up there?" Tianna asked, closing the door behind them.

Shannon pulled an aluminum ladder from behind the clothes hanging on the rod.

"Didn't Mary ever see it?" Tianna asked, surprised.

"She underestimates me all the time," Shannon replied, starting up the rungs. "She probably thinks I use it to get my clothes down off their hangers. She confuses sick with stupid."

Tianna felt like a dolt. It had taken her forever to discover that Mary was an impostor, but Shannon seemed to have figured it out easily. She followed her up the ladder, nervous that Mary's telepathic hold was becoming stronger. Soon Mary would realize she'd been tricked and would return.

She poked her head into the attic. It wasn't as dark as she had expected under the pitched roof. Three dirt-streaked dormer windows let in hazy light. She pulled herself through the opening. The smells of dust and mildew settled over her, but there was also a sweet fragrance that didn't belong. Using her telekinetic power, she lifted the ladder, set it aside, then closed the trapdoor.

A match flared behind her and she turned.

Shannon lit a scented candle and then another, until flickering flames shot light over the red, white, gold, and blue Tibetan prayer flags hanging from the crossbeams. The fire's glow was reflected in the serene images of saints and prophets that encircled Shannon. The statue of Ganesha sat together with several sculptures of the Buddha.

Carefully, Tianna stepped over prayer cards, rosaries, and a crucifix set on a purple cloth. As soon as she crossed into the ring of candles, her telepathic connection to Mary was severed.

"Why so many different religions?" Tianna asked.

"When my mom was still alive, she said God gave us lots of roads to find peace, like a mountain, you know, with more than one way to the top. I figured I needed more help than most people." She looked suddenly thin and ashen.

"How long have you been coming up here?" Tianna sat beside her and placed an arm around her.

"Since I saw Mary become a shadow. I would have told you sooner about my secret place, but I didn't know if I could trust you, because you do weird things, too." Shannon had seen Tianna use her power.

The sound of muffled footsteps interrupted their conversation. The closet door below them opened with a gentle squeak. Shannon clutched Tianna's hand, her eyes widening with fear.

"Shannon," Mary called in a soft voice, her tone so compelling that Tianna was afraid Shannon might answer.

But the next time Mary called out, her voice seemed farther away. Tianna listened, wondering why Mary hadn't turned to shadow and glided up to their hiding place. Maybe Shannon in her innocence had created a magic room. Maggie had said the Atrox was unable to feel love and was therefore blind to anything hidden in loving thoughts. Now Tianna wondered if Mary was unable to sense their presence because the sacred images in the attic concealed them in a circle of love.

They sat in silence for a long while, and when the house became quiet again, Tianna asked, "Did you ever try to tell anyone what was going on?"

"I told Dr. Reeves, but he figured my medication was making me hallucinate. He told Mary everything I'd said. Can you image that?" Shannon's frail body seemed to tremble in reaction to the memory. Then she spoke with anger. "I knew what I saw, but I'd been in the system long enough to know I had to go along with what Mary said. I just pretended it had been my medicine."

Tianna understood at once. Sometimes foster homes were good, but other times survival meant buying into the family's peculiar sense of reality and agreeing with them no matter what your own judgment told you was true.

"I started spying on her then, and after you came to live with us, I sometimes got a creepy feeling that she was invisible and watching us to see if I'd tell you anything." Shannon started to say more, but a barely audible sound made her pause.

Tianna tilted her head, listening. Stealthy footsteps crept into the bedroom, followed by an odd clattering. Voices whispered in the closet below them. Had Mary found them after all?

The trapdoor opened.

CHAPTER TWENTY-ONE

SERENA POKED THROUGH the opening into the attic. She stood on a rickety wooden ladder, the top step covered with dirt and cobwebs. Her hair was braided into thick pigtails, and her face was now clean of makeup. The flannel collar of her pajamas stuck out from under her sweatshirt. "Tianna? Why are you in the attic?"

"Serena?" Tianna answered, feeling grateful and surprised. "How did you know to find me here?"

"Stanton told me you were in trouble, so we came to help." She glanced around, her eyes widening as she took in Shannon's altar. The flapping candle flames were reflected in her pupils.

Catty pushed against Serena, trying to see inside. She had changed from her party clothes and now wore blue sweats with the image of a skull and crossbones on the front. The skull was adorned with a large pink bow.

"We've been prowling through the house trying to find you," Catty said. "We didn't know what to think. Your front door was open, and it didn't look like anyone was home, but Serena sensed your thoughts and said you were up here. Lucky for you, we found this ladder outside by the garage, or we never would have had a way to get you down."

Tianna felt tremendous relief, but at the same time a new worry swept through her. Where had Mary gone? She wouldn't just suddenly leave unless she had had a good reason. Could this have been yet another attempt to ensnare all the Daughters?

"What happened?" Serena asked.

"Mary turned out to be a Follower," Tianna replied as she helped Shannon onto the ladder.

"Sweet, perfect Mary?" Catty asked with surprise as she stepped onto the closet floor. She still wore her monkey-face slippers and her striped socks.

"Hey, Tianna." Vanessa waited at the bottom, balancing the ladder. Her hair was pinned up in curls and held in place with big plastic clips. She'd thrown a coat over her nightgown and wore untied tennis shoes. "Tell us more about Mary. What was going on?"

"It's like all her energy went into keeping up a facade of the perfect woman," Tianna explained as they followed her back to her room. When she had finished telling them everything that had happened, she picked up her backpack and added, "I should have left L.A. a long time ago. I'm going now, tonight."

"You can't," Serena said. "You have to stay."

"It's too dangerous," Tianna answered.

Vanessa held her tightly. "When it's safe,

send a postcard, or call, so we can get together again."

"I will," Tianna promised, knowing that she wouldn't. She sensed she'd never see them again. Then she caught Serena's expression and knew that Serena felt the same way.

"This is good-bye for real, isn't it?" Catty said.

Tianna nodded, then hugged each one of them. At last she unclasped her moon amulet and fastened it around Shannon's neck. "You keep it. You're more goddess than I am. I'm just a street kid with the weird ability to move things."

Then she looked back at the others. "Take care of Shannon for me."

Catty put an arm around her. "Maybe Kendra can become her foster mom. She needs someone who isn't always in trouble like me."

"How do you know I'm not always in trouble?" Shannon snapped.

Her response pleased Catty, and she gave her a wild hug. "You're a perfect sister for me."

Tianna hesitated. It still troubled her

that they didn't know where Mary was. "Leave quickly," she whispered, by way of farewell. "I don't understand why Mary hasn't come back."

"Maybe the Atrox made her an outcast when she let you escape," Serena said, as if she knew.

"She's probably hanging out with Justin and Mason now." Vanessa smirked.

"You go," Catty urged. "We'll pack some things for Shannon and leave right away."

Tianna nodded and ran down the stairs, but as she started out the doorway she remembered the vitamins. Mary had said they were a potion. She ran back to the kitchen, grabbed a bottle, shook out a few tablets, stuffed them in her pocket, and then rushed outside.

She picked up her skateboard, rolled it in front of her, jumped on, and started down the street. As the wheels clicked over the seams in the sidewalk, her body started to relax. She shifted her weight to the right to turn the corner, and a sudden movement caught her eye. Without warning, two men leaped from the shadows and grabbed her. She kicked and squirmed. Her attackers weren't Followers, just hoodlums, and Ethan's nasty face flashed across her mind. She summoned her power, but before she could release it, they threw her into the back of a van. Her head hit metal flooring with a clank, and something sharp in her backpack poked her spine.

The doors slammed shut with an echoing twang, and the men jumped into the front. The engine roared, and the driver took the corner too quickly. The van slid sideways, tilting on two wheels, and then the tires came back and caught the road with an ear-piercing squeal.

Tianna and her kidnappers sped into the night.

CHAPTER TWENTY-TWO

THE BRUISES ON Tianna's arm still ached, and now she had a knot on the back of her head, maybe even a concussion, to judge by the way it throbbed. She groaned and gradually became aware of the smells of spices and onions. She opened her eyes and stared at the framed photograph of an unsmiling couple posed stiffly and staring straight at the camera.

"You like my wedding picture," a familiar voice said. "I was so young then."

Tianna turned abruptly, and intense pain shot across her forehead.

Madame Oskar sat propped on a cozy stack of pillows near the rear doors. The plain curtains over the back windows flapped back and forth, and the streetlights fluttered over her tranquil face. She held up a glass filled with clear brown liquid and strawberries.

"Romani tea," she said as if this had been an everyday social visit. "Do you want some?"

Tianna shook her head and opened her backpack. She shook two aspirin from the bottle, tossed them into her mouth, and swallowed. The bitter taste lingered on the back of her tongue. Then she flexed each foot, testing her bones, and cautiously sat up. She still felt dizzy and gingerly rubbed the lump on her skull.

Madame explained. "My sons were anxious to get you into the van before you could use your power on them. I'm sorry. They're good boys. Students at UCLA."

"Why did you kidnap me?" Tianna asked

indignantly, surprised that Madame was her abductor, but also relieved.

"The day you walked into my shop, you became my responsibility." Madame Oskar slipped a strawberry into her mouth.

"Why is that?" Tianna eased around a basket filled with casserole dishes wrapped in aluminum foil and sat on a velvet cushion next to Madame.

"Good and evil forces are fighting over you," Madame said simply.

"You saw that in your crystal ball?" Tianna asked, mystified; her trust, however, was now stronger than her doubt.

"I don't have any magical powers to see the future. If I did, I'd be living in a castle." Madame laughed, the sound soft and comforting. "Fortune-telling is a way to make an income."

"But you told me—"

"I was trying to convince you to come with me, and obviously, you should have listened. I've always been open to the Good in the universe; I sensed what you were when I saw you, and then you used your powers and I knew."

"What am I?" Tianna held her breath.

"If the forces for Good in the universe don't want you to remember, should I tell you?" Madame sniffed as if she detected a strange odor in the air.

"I suppose not," Tianna said, but frustration made her restless.

Madame patted her hand, her fingers warm from the tea. "This coming dawn marks the beginning of your last day unless you can escape. You had to leave Los Angeles, so we came back to get you."

"I was going on my own," Tianna countered, exhausted and wanting to rest.

"Do you really think you could have gotten out of Los Angeles without protection?" She lifted the curtain with the tips of her fingers.

The sky blazed with raven-black lightning, and for the first time the low vibration of thunder rumbled through the air.

"The storm is coming closer," Madame Oskar's son called from the front seat. The engine shuddered as he pressed his foot harder on the accelerator.

"We'll take you to Baker," Madame said. "You can go anywhere from there."

Tianna imagined herself starting a new life in the small high desert town. "Maybe I could stay there."

"I have your bus ticket already." She handed Tianna a cross-country pass and sniffed again. She stared at Tianna as if something had triggered a bad memory. "That smell. Do you have something with you?"

Tianna pulled the vitamins from her pocket and displayed them in her palm. "My foster mom was—"

Before she could finish, Madame set her tea aside, kicked the backdoors open, grabbed the pills, and threw them out. Capsules and tablets bounced on the asphalt, illuminated by the headlights of the car behind them like a sudden miniature hailstorm.

"I wanted to find out what they were," Tianna said, exasperated. "Now I'll never know."

"They were a danger for you!" Madame leaned out and yanked the door handle. Her long hair flew up and around her head, and when she slammed the door the black strands fell to her shoulders. She settled back inside. "The pills contained potions with transmutative powers to change all the goodness the goddess Selene has put into you."

"Change it into what?" Tianna demanded.

"Evil," Madame whispered, her eyes wide and knowing.

Tianna thought of Todd, and her heart clenched. "Is there an antidote?"

"I'm sorry," Madame said, as if sensing her grief. She went on: "You must look to the future now and forget the past. You'll start again on the *lungo drom*, the long road. That's what your life will be. There's no turning back now."

"To wander forever?" Tianna asked, exhausted. "That's what you expect me to do?"

Madame shook her head. "That suggests aimlessness and lack of purpose. You have a reason—an urgent one. As for me and my sons, we'd prefer to stay settled in our home and keep our jobs, but now our lives have been interrupted by a more important purpose."

"To keep me from my destiny," Tianna muttered, her chest hollow, already missing Los Angeles and her friends.

The van rattled and shimmied onto the freeway, then found an even rhythm. Within an hour they were chugging up the Cajon Pass. Tianna's ears became plugged up because of the change in altitude. She closed her eyes, but she felt too overwrought to sleep.

When they reached the high desert, Madame seemed to relax. She took casseroles from the basket and passed out cabbage rolls to her sons and Tianna, then served potatoes stuffed with jelly for dessert.

Soon after, as gray dawn broke over the vast stretch of Mojave Desert, they pulled into a vacant lot next to a gas station. Madame crawled out and gazed reverently at the eastern sky, as if summoning the morning sun, and then she and Tianna sat under the prickly branches of a Joshua tree and waited. Madame Oskar's sons stood guard nearby.

Soon after, a Greyhound bus swayed onto

the lot. The big wheels crunched gravel and stones, raising a storm of dust. The doors opened with a swish of air. The driver jumped out to open up the baggage compartment, but stopped when he saw that Tianna carried only a backpack. He took her ticket and jumped back on board.

"Bye." Tianna started up the steps.

Madame pulled her back and tied a red thread around her wrist. "This is the *loli dori*. Normally it's tied to an infant to protect the child from *jakhalo*, the evil eye, but you'll wear it now and go, with my blessing and my love."

Madame kissed her and held her for a long moment.

Tianna reluctantly pulled away and boarded the bus. She found a place near the back and turned to wave good-bye from the window, but the van was already speeding from the lot, sand spinning in its trail.

The coach rocked back and forth as Tianna settled into her seat, wondering what her future held. The desolate landscape hurried by, all bronze sand and sun-blackened craggy hills. She tried to make sense of everything Madame Oskar had told her, but the dry winds whistled against the window, singing an eerie lullaby, and she fell asleep wondering why good and evil forces were fighting over her.

She awakened hours later, her heart hammering with fear. She had slept the day away. The sun was setting, and long shadows stretched across the land. She vaguely remembered stopping in several different towns.

With a start she realized she was resting against someone's shoulder. She turned to apologize, and stared into Ethan's eyes.

CHAPTER TWENTY-THREE

"Ethan?" Tianna jerked back, stunned, and adrenaline flooded through her. She pressed against the window to get as far from him as she could.

"You don't need to be afraid of me," he said, amused. "I've been following you for a long time now."

Her heart skidded into panic, and her power

shot out wrong. The seat back in front of her began to smolder. She strained to keep her
energy contained, terrified she might harm other
passengers.

"Do you always attack before finding out if
someone is on your side?" Ethan crushed the
small flame with his palm, and the acrid smell of
smoke stirred the air. "I could be your guardian
angel."

Was he? She wished she had her amulet now.
She didn't sense evil emanating from him. Perhaps
like people, angels had diverse personalities.

"Just my luck," she blurted. "Other girls get
heavenly creatures with halos, and I get a loser."

"Maybe I'm not as bad as you think." A mysterious smile crossed his face, and he slipped on a
black fedora. The turned-down brim hid his eyes.

"You're the one from my dreams." She stared
at him, spellbound. Could he be her protector?

"You thought you dreamed my presence," he
explained. "But we've been together, night after
night."

"But why—"

His thought interrupted her: *Don't you know who you are yet, Tianna?*

He took her hand and she let him. The red thread Madame had given her was no longer tied around her wrist. Had he taken it? She started to ask but stopped, captivated. His fingers ran over her palm and her body turned traitor, responding to his touch. She stared, mesmerized, wanting to stay with him forever. He had to be a Follower to do this to her.

I'm not a Follower! The words burst through her and awakened the pain in her head, back, and arms. Whatever spell he had cast over her ruptured, and her power burst free in a pandemonium of sparks. She suppressed her energy, but it slithered, snakelike, under her skin, trying to get out.

"Let it explode." Ethan smoothed his finger down her cheek. His caress sent a pleasant shiver through her. "I can feel your power shimmering near the surface. It's unnatural for you to hold it in. You were created to destroy."

A sudden image broke into her mind of

exploding buildings. She saw herself walking down Wilshire Boulevard amid the rubble, blasting cars, clothing stores, and taco stands. Was that her destiny, to tear down everything in her path? Each of the Daughters had a powerful dark side. Did she have one, too? She must have.

"Free yourself," he said soothingly. "When your power finds no outlet, it turns on you. You've repressed it too long, and now it wants to become its own entity, with you as its vessel."

She caught her breath, remembering the invisible hands. "But I don't want to hurt anyone."

"You've seen your potential," he encouraged. "Release it. Show the world your power before your power dominates you."

She could feel him in her thoughts now, enjoying her struggle to stop the storm inside her. Finally, she conquered her telekinetic energy and put it to rest.

"Didn't you ever wonder why you're so much stronger than the other Daughters?" He caressed her side.

"How can I be? I wasn't born a Daughter,"

she said, no longer surprised by anything he knew about her.

"I know. You're much more than a goddess." He folded his arms around her and drew her to him.

She didn't resist. She closed her eyes and tilted her head, waiting for his kiss, but instead of a warm embrace, she felt a chill shoot through her. Her eyes flashed open. She sensed her body fading and knew intuitively he was taking her back to L. A.

"Please don't. I can't return." She didn't fear Ethan as much as L.A. and the destiny that waited for her there. "Any place else. I'll go with you gladly."

"Too late," he whispered, his face turning to smoke.

His shady silhouette entwined itself around her and she became a black vapor, mingling with his; then they glided like a blur of night along the floor of the bus. He slipped through a crack in the window and pulled her with him out into the darkness. Wind screamed around them, lifting them high into the air. The scent of sagebrush melded with her own, and she became aware of each nocturnal creature rustling through the scrub oaks below.

The moonlit stretch of land swept beneath them, and then they rose above the jagged San Gabriel Mountains, a streak of murky cloud. At last, Ethan dove toward the San Fernando Valley and slowed their flight. Treetops tickled through her with the rich taste of pine and then, down again they went, flat against the land. They surged over oil-stained freeways and sped past cars. The thick fumes choked her.

With a sudden jolt, Tianna's feet hit black-top, and she slammed back into her body. She gasped for air and blinked, then staggered away from Ethan, dizzy and cold, the taste of automobile exhaust strong on her tongue. She spit, feeling nauseated, and Ethan caught her before she fell.

They had materialized on the campus of La Brea High School, near the music room. The wind sighed mournfully through the twisting corridors, and in the dim light the graffiti on the stucco walls looked like hieroglyphs in an ancient tomb.

Tianna eased away from Ethan, already intent on breaking free. If she could borrow money for an airline ticket she could still leave L. A. that night. Her heartbeat accelerated in anticipation of her escape, but before she could take another step, Ethan clasped her arm. With one glance into his dark eyes she knew he had caught her plan before she had even completed her thought.

"I'm your guardian," he whispered, his imperious tone implying he would always be with her. "There is no escape." Then he lifted his hand and released her.

She hesitated, wondering why he was letting her go. Had he brought her here only so the Atrox could finish its deadly game? Or was he truly a guardian angel, but one sent by the Fates to bring her back to L. A. to live out her cruel destiny?

CHAPTER TWENTY-FOUR

Tianna sprinted recklessly down the corridor outside the empty classrooms. Her boots hammered the concrete walkway, and the noise echoed around her. An ominous change had taken over the night, and when she burst onto the tarmac in front of the school, the starry sky seemed to press down on her, as if the universe were about to collapse.

She lunged at the security fence. Her fingers

caught the rough metal, and she climbed up and swung her leg over the top, snagging the cuff of her jeans on the spiky wires. She tugged, and the chain-link mesh swung dangerously back and forth.

At last, she ripped free and jumped. She landed in a squat, and pain shot up her spine. She pushed off in a feverish run toward Derek's house.

Derek had broken up with her, but she knew she could rely on him still. She only hoped he had money left to lend her; then maybe she could be in Portland or Seattle later that night. If not, she hoped he'd at least drive her up the coast to Ventura or maybe even as far as Santa Barbara. She prayed he'd run away with her.

Her throat burned from breathing through her mouth, but she didn't slow her pace. She darted across a newly mowed lawn. The automatic sprinklers turned on, and the smell of wet earth and grass surged into the air. She leaped over a short hedge and headed down another street lined with thick, gnarled trees.

On the next block, branches creaked and swayed unnaturally. Her telekinetic power had formed a ring of motion around her, taunting her with its rebellion. Leaves swept about her in a blustering gale. She concentrated and stopped the movement. Her power cramped inside her and fought, ricocheting about, looking for escape. It seemed emboldened, and when it couldn't find a way to free itself, it purred contentedly beneath her skin, as if it sensed her losing the race.

Tall hedges hid Derek's front porch in shadow. She hurried down his walk, crossed the wide veranda, and rang the doorbell. Resting her hands on her knees, she leaned over, trying to catch her breath.

Muffled sounds came from inside as if someone were peering through the peephole. The porch light turned on.

Tianna winced at the sudden brightness, but when the door still didn't open, she stood and pounded on the wood. "Derek! Let me in."

The latch turned and Corrine peered out.

"Tianna?" Corinne's voice had lost its smugness, and she seemed unsure of herself.

"Where's Derek?" Tianna shoved inside, ignoring the sinking feeling in her chest. What was Corrine doing there? She stopped. The silence felt too deep. Something was missing, and then she knew. The steady ticking of the pendulum in the grandfather clock wasn't echoing down the hallway like it usually did. She pushed around Corrine and headed toward the family room, terrified by what she might see.

"Don't leave me," Corrine cried from behind her, her feet slapping against the tiled floor.

Tianna almost tripped over the fallen clock. The rope chain and weights had been torn from the base and used to smash the face. She turned abruptly, then stepped over the mahogany case. "Derek?"

When there was no answer, she crept into the room. The drapes were open, and through the sliding glass door she could see the swimming pool. The lights shimmered beneath the water and reflected across the ceiling in meandering waves.

Derek sat on the couch in black jeans and a white tee, watching the television. The sound was muted, and his lips moved as if he were reading the captions sweeping across the bottom of the screen. A bowl of popcorn sat on the coffee table next to his car keys and a copy of *National Geographic*.

Tianna stepped closer. The glow from the TV fluttered over his listless face. His back drooped, as if something had crushed his spirit, and his watch lay broken at his feet.

Then Tianna remembered something Maggie had once told her: *Followers hate timepieces—anything that reminds them of their eternal bond to evil.* Tianna picked up the pieces of the broken watch. She plopped onto the couch, too weary to stand, suddenly overwhelmed by unbearable sadness.

Corrine switched on the overhead fluorescent lights, and a harsh glare flooded the room.

Derek turned with sluggish slowness and looked at Tianna as if he were about to cry. He had an odd darkness in his eyes, like a sliver of night, rather than the usual yellow glint of a Follower's eyes.

Tianna placed a reassuring hand on his arm, but he cringed as if her touch were unbearable.

"I found him this way." Corrine grabbed an orange afghan, wrapped it around her shoulders, and sat on the edge of an ottoman. Her legs trembled beneath her long skirt, and she gripped her knees, but it didn't stop the shaking.

That was when Tianna noticed the bitterly cold sting in the air. She huffed, and her breath turned to white vapor. "What happened?"

"I came over to watch videos." Corrine's cheeks grew pallid, as if the memory were leaching life from her. "The front door was open, so I walked in. At first I thought my eyes were only adjusting to the dark, but it was like walking into black velvet and—"

"The Atrox," Derek cut in, his expression dead.

"That's the first he's spoken." Corrine stared at him. "What's the Atrox?"

Tianna shrugged, and turned her attention back to Derek. He looked confused and wounded. The Atrox had stolen his hope, sucked it from his soul, and now, unless she did something, Derek would become a predator himself, stealing hope from others in order to replenish his own and feel alive again. But why would the Atrox do something usually left to Followers?

Maybe it had to do with her *becoming*. She couldn't consider the reason now. She had to get the Daughters together. They could bring Derek back. They had saved others countless times before, and she prayed they could do it again, but she had to act quickly.

"Stay with him, Corrine." She started to stand but Derek clasped her hand, his fingers icy.

Strange, sputtering sounds came from his throat, and his lips twisted, trying to form the words. "The Daughters," he said hoarsely.

"Daughters?" Corrine asked and sniffled. "What is he talking about now?"

"What about them?" Tianna tenderly touched his cheek, coaxing him to continue. She could feel the fatal cold inside him. "Tell me."

"Warn them—" he whispered, but before he could finish, an odd humming gathered in the air.

It resonated about them until a shrill noise filled the room and the walls trembled.

"Is it an earthquake?" Corrine pressed her hands over her ears.

The glass in the sliding door rattled wildly.

A thin whistle escaped Tianna's lungs. Was her energy on a rampage again? She hadn't felt it discharge, but if she hadn't caused this, then what had? She started to rope her power back but suddenly realized it lay curled inside her, asleep. She scanned the dark corners and the unlit hallway. Was the Atrox still present and trying to keep Derek from speaking?

"What do I need to tell the Daughters?" She grabbed his shoulders.

In reply the window buckled and exploded. Corrine ran to her and huddled against her as thousands of glass shards shot across the room and rained down on them.

"The Atrox is coming!" Derek warned, but his eyes were unfocused, as if he were looking at something only he could see. He didn't even seem aware of the broken glass on his lap or the blood streaming down his cheek in tiny rivulets.

"Is something coming after us?" Corrine asked, her voice sliding into panic.

"Put the cello down and run!" Derek yelled.

"Cello," Tianna repeated and understood at once that Derek had a telepathic connection to the Atrox; he was able to see what it saw.

"Go! Get out!" he shouted.

"Watch him," she said to Corrine. She knew with dead certainty that Serena was in danger, and she had only minutes to get to her house and warn her. "I'm taking his car."

Corrine nodded and pieces of glass fell from her hair and bounced off the coffee table.

Tianna scooped up the car keys and bolted toward the door, her boots crunching over broken glass. She vaulted over the fallen clock and ran outside. She hated to leave Derek and Corrine alone, but she couldn't worry about them right now. If the Atrox destroyed all the Daughters, the world as it was now would end. Even if it captured only one Daughter, the powers of the others would be weakened.

She jumped into Derek's car and turned the key in the ignition. The engine roared and she dropped the gearshift into reverse and backed out of the long driveway. She braked, slipped into drive, then slammed her foot on the gas pedal and shot down the street. She leaned over the steering wheel and stared up through the windshield at the sky, searching for the moon. Where was her guiding light?

At last she found a crescent slice of white, just before an ominous black cloud eclipsed it. She had always loved the magic in the night, but now, without the lunar glow, she felt the Atrox pulsing in the air. It controlled the evil forces in the world, and those forces were strongest without the moon.

"*O Mater Luna, Regina nocis, adiuvo me nunc.*" The prayer was only said in times of grave danger, but when she whispered the words now, they gave little comfort.

Minutes later, she rammed her foot on the brake, opened the driver's door, and jumped out. The front tires rolled up over the curb and the car stopped, the engine racing. Blue clouds choked from the tailpipe.

She rushed up the walkway and pounded on Serena's door, feeling too jumpy to stand on the unlit porch for long. A sudden gust made her turn, and she studied the shadows spreading over the lawn. Tree branches swished back and forth in a quickening breeze, and, up and down the street, leaves fluttered with the same haunting vibration. Her power couldn't have created such a stirring. It had to be the wind—unless her energy was growing, becoming boundless, and preparing her for her destiny.

"Serena!" She banged on the door until it swung open.

"Tianna?" Collin stood in front of her, bewildered, holding Wally, Serena's pet raccoon. "Serena said you'd left Los Angeles to prevent a disaster. What are you doing back?"

"I need to talk to her," she said quickly and jostled past him.

He closed the door behind them. "She isn't home." An odd paleness spread beneath his tan, as if his body sensed something tragically wrong before his mind had even perceived it.

"Where'd she go?" Tianna asked, her uneasiness growing.

"I don't know. Maybe she's with Stanton." He shrugged, but a disturbing look crossed his face. "She was practicing her cello—"

"No!" Tianna yelled and ran blindly down the gloomy hallway.

Collin trailed after her.

Despair gripped her; she knew she was too late, but she dashed through the dining room anyway. Her power rushed ahead of her, toppling a chair, and then it pushed against the swinging door and held it open. She darted into the kitchen and stopped.

The air was unbearably cold, and her teeth began to chatter. Papers lay scattered across the floor. The cello had fallen on its side, the end pin broken. She kept a chokehold on her energy. It wanted to burst free and express her grief with wild destruction. Invisible hands tickled her shoulders, as if searching for a handhold.

Immediately she took a deep breath and quelled her power, reining it in until she had control again.

Collin set Wally down on the floor and picked up the tattered pieces of the *Ramayana*.

"I've been reading this," he said quietly, flipping through the torn pages. "It's about gods reincarnating and coming back to earth as warriors in order to destroy demons. I thought it might help me understand what was happening to Jimena."

The book slipped from his fingers, and he fell into a chair, looking drained. "The Atrox took Serena, didn't it?"

"Maybe," Tianna answered, afraid that it had. She glimpsed the kitchen clock. It was past nine already. She needed to hurry.

"Call Vanessa and Catty!" she shouted. "Warn them the Atrox is coming."

Collin lifted the receiver even as she spoke, but when he held it to his ear, his forehead wrinkled in a scowl. "The line is dead."

She didn't bother to wait while he tried his

cell phone. She knew that it would be useless as well. She ran from the house, bolted down the walk, then jumped into Derek's car, turned the steering wheel and slammed her foot on the gas pedal.

The car lunged off the curb, then skidded before catching the road and speeding away. She buckled her seatbelt as her energy trembled through her, demanding its freedom. She could feel it becoming stronger than her will to hold it back. She swallowed hard and tried to find the moon in the ebony sky. She saw nothing and pressed her foot harder. The car accelerated, breaking the speed limit. She kept her hand on the horn and raced through stop signs.

Less than ten minutes later, Tianna stood on Vanessa's front porch, knocking on the door. She sensed danger, but then Vanessa's mother answered and stood in front of her, holding a cup of coffee, as if it were an ordinary night.

"Hi, Tianna. Vanessa's not home." She smiled brightly, then caught Tianna's eyes, and her face tensed. "Where's Vanessa?" She clutched Tianna's shoulders, her fingers digging deep. "What happened to my Vanessa?"

Tianna shook her head and tried to force a smile. Vanessa's mother knew nothing about the Daughters. She didn't have a clue.

"I'm only looking for her," Tianna lied and glanced at the drive. Vanessa's red Mustang was parked in the garage. "Maybe she went out with Michael and the band."

"Maybe." Her mother nodded, but her eyes bimmed with tears. "I just got home and I didn't see a note."

Thunder ricocheted across the sky and the wind began to blow. Palm fronds rustled overhead and Vanessa's mother walked out onto the lawn. She stood next to the twisted olive tree, apprehension gathering on her face as she searched the churning sky.

"We haven't had a thunderstorm for ages." She stared at the gathering clouds, her brown hair blowing into her eyes. "I wish Vanessa were home." She turned to Tianna, her eyes imploring. "Find her for me. I need her here before the storm comes."

"I'll find her," Tianna promised, but her words felt like a lie. If the Atrox had captured both Serena and Vanessa, what chance did she and Catty have of freeing them? Jimena's powers were strong, but they couldn't rely on her yet. She was too confused by her new identity.

Exhausted, Tianna slumped back inside the car. She twisted the steering wheel and did a huge, looping turn, then jetted down the street, sensing something worse than a tempest stirring outside the car. Black bolts of lightning throbbed across the sky. Afterimages of the jagged spikes stung her eyes. She blinked. How could darkness be so bright?

Distant sirens filled the night and she knew intuitively that the emergency vehicles were heading toward Catty's house. Moments later she stopped at the corner. Blue police lights flashed in a jittery pattern over houses and the faces of curious neighbors gathered on the lawn. Kendra stood on the front porch under a beam of pale light, her face haunted. She spoke to two police officer and cradled Shannon against her side.

Another officer walked the yard, unrolling yellow tape to mark off the crime scene. What had happened?

Nausea choked Tianna. She didn't really want to know. She sensed that the capture of the Daughters was inextricably related to her *becoming*. Madame Oskar had said good and evil forces were fighting over her, but why was she so important? Her last hope was Jimena.

Abruptly she turned the steering wheel and jammed the gas pedal to the floor. The engine sputtered, shaking violently, and died. She sighed, defeated. Without a car, how could she reach Jimena in time?

CHAPTER TWENTY-FIVE

Black lightning scorched the sky, and jagged bolts scattered into the clouds. The night became incandescent, and the shadows radiated an eerie red glow. Immediately, thunder boomed and rocked the earth, the vibration shaking through Tianna's chest. The moon peeked from behind a shroud of gloomy mist, and she was overcome with a feeling near panic. She abandoned the car in the middle of the street and started running, her breath ragged.

Wind slashed around her, bending trees. People had gathered on their porches and in their doorways to watch the storm.

Another shock of lightning crackled, illuminating the dark with ebony fire, and in the throbbing light Tianna glimpsed the shuddering outline of a bicycle leaning against a porch railing. She rushed across the lawn and grabbed the handlebars, ignoring the man and two boys in the window, pounding on it and warning her away.

"I'm only borrowing it!" Tianna yelled and shot them a look.

The man grabbed his children and stepped away from the glass, fear in his eyes. What had he seen in her face to make him so afraid?

She couldn't consider it now. She wheeled the bike onto the sidewalk, swung on and started pedaling at breakneck speed.

When she reached La Brea Boulevard she launched off the curb into traffic. The front fender of a Cadillac grazed her knee. She shot her power out and the car slammed to a stop, the bumper crumpling as if it had hit a wall. The startled driver fell against his seatbelt; then his head jerked back and his hand hit the horn, honking at her. She ignored him and whipped away, weaving around cars stopped for the traffic light.

Sweat dripped from her forehead in spite of the cold wind, and adrenaline surged through her in a steady flow, making her senses hyperalert. Her hair flapped wildly behind her and she breathed in the night, her power hissing inside her. She felt more warrior than goddess in this surreal storm. If her bike had turned into a galloping steed she wouldn't have been surprised.

She took Wilshire Boulevard against the light. Cars screeched to a stop, barely missing her. She hunched over the handlebars and pedaled furiously past the Los Angeles County Art Museum. Her lungs burned and her legs screamed.

Cautiously she let out her telekinetic energy. It strained like a vicious dog against her control, but she bent it to her need. In her mind's eye she imagined invisible hands pushing her forward. Soon she was passing cars, the bike tires smoking from the friction of being propelled across the asphalt faster than the wheels could turn.

Within minutes she swerved onto the lawn in front of the apartment building where Jimena lived. She jumped off the bike and let it fall. The acrid smell of burning rubber drifted into the air.

She sprinted up the walk and tried to open the door with her mind, but she had exhausted her power, and fatigue made it twist out wrong. The stone lion on the right side of the porch exploded, sending chunks of granite clattering around her as she took the steps two at a time. She pressed the intercom button, leaning her body against her thumb.

"I've been waiting for you, Tianna." Jimena's voice came through the speaker and at the same time the magnetic lock buzzed and opened.

Tianna grabbed the doorknob and ran inside. She ignored the elevator, too afraid she might lose control inside the metal box, and bounded up the stairs instead, then sprinted down the hallway.

Jimena was waiting for her at the entrance to

her grandmother's small apartment, dressed in a robe, her hair flowing over her shoulders.

"The Atrox has Serena, Catty, and Vanessa," Tianna muttered, through gasps for air. "At least I think it does."

Jimena wrapped a comforting arm around her and hurried her inside, her black eyes anxious, as if she understood what Tianna had been through.

"I saw the Atrox in *el cielo*," Jimena whispered. "It's acting as if it owns the night already, the way it's flaunting itself in the sky, and it isn't even midnight."

"What happens then?" Tianna asked and for the first time she noticed how much Jimena had changed. She radiated with an inner glow, her eyes piercing and astonishingly beautiful.

"The outcome is still unknown." Jimena stepped into the kitchen. She sat at the small table and stared out the window above the sink.

Wind shrieked against the glass, rattling the panes as if evil forces were demanding entry. Hellish lightning flashed, and strange shadows shuddered across the picture of the Virgin of Guadalupe hanging on the wall.

Tianna slouched into the chair across from Jimena and gratefully kicked off her boots. She rubbed her sore feet. "How are we going to get them back?"

"*Tengo que decirte algo.*" Jimena leaned forward, her eyes downcast. "There's something I need to tell you first."

"What could be more important than getting them back?" Tianna asked, ready to argue, then stopped. "Did your memories return?"

Jimena nodded. "*No mucho.* Not all, but some." Her face tightened with grief, and her fingers absently turned the brown pottery bowl that was filled with salsa. The spicy scent of peppers and onions drifted into the air.

"Fifteen years ago," she began slowly, "Selene stole a baby from the Atrox. She gave the infant to one of her Daughters to rear. The Daughter was turning seventeen and had bravely asked to make the change. The metamorphosis doesn't always involve turning into a spiritual form. In rare cases it means taking on a difficult duty or an impossible challenge, and keeping one's goddess powers and memories."

Tianna nodded impatiently, trying to get Jimena to hurry.

"Selene needed to protect the child from her destiny, and the Daughter accepted the responsibility of rearing the baby as her transformation. She succeeded far beyond anyone's hopes. The child grew strong and good. That little girl was you."

"My mother was a goddess, a Daughter of the Moon?" Tianna gasped, and then the meaning of what Jimena had said hit her. "You mean my real parents gave me to the Atrox when I was only an infant?" Tianna held her breath, then let it out, trying to comprehend. Her heart was thumping heavily. "Why? Were they Followers?"

"No one gave you to the Atrox," Jimena explained, her voice grim.

"The Atrox stole me, the way it stole Stanton?" Tianna gasped, feeling a selfish surge of hope. Already her mind was rushing forward, wondering if she had brothers and sisters, and where they lived. "Do you know who my real parents are?"

"Yes," Jimena answered mysteriously, but her scowl made Tianna nervous.

"Are they dead, too?" Tianna asked uneasily.

"Dejame explicar," Jimena said somberly. "Let me explain. In the beginning of ancient time, Zeus asked Hephaestus to create the perfect woman."

"Pandora," Tianna interrupted, flustered. She couldn't bear to hear a story now. "Tell me later. I want to know about my parents."

"I am telling you," Jimena insisted. *"Escuchame.* Listen to me."

Tianna sat back, seething, and glanced at the small clock on the wall. It was almost eleven. She folded her arms over her chest and glared at Jimena.

"Hephaestus sculpted a woman so beautiful no man could resist her," Jimena continued, frowning. "The Atrox carefully watched him work the clay, and when he had finished, the Atrox made plans to steal Pandora."

"Selene stopped the Atrox," Tianna broke in, her patience exhausted. "I've heard that story a hundred times."

"There's a lot you haven't heard," Jimena said, ignoring Tianna's outburst. "When Selene stopped the Atrox from abducting Pandora, it vowed to learn how to create the breath of life and make its own irresistibly beautiful woman. Throughout the centuries it has had countless failures, many monstrous outcomes—"

"What happened to them?" Tianna asked, curious now, and feeling unexpected compassion for the creatures.

"Most live in Nefandus, the Atrox's realm," Jimena said. "Some are Regulators, and a few, like Mary, try to live in our world."

"Mary?" Tianna's hatred for Mary suddenly fell away, replaced by a terrible pity. "But what does that have to do with what's happening now?"

"You were its first success," Jimena said finally. "The Atrox created you."

CHAPTER TWENTY-SIX

JIMENA'S WORDS HUNG between them as if they had a power of their own. Tianna slumped back in her chair. Her chest froze and her stomach knotted, and then something let go, and she no longer felt connected to this world. Dark clouds pushed into her vision and a cry exploded from her lungs. Her energy swirled about, matching her dizziness, and rattled the statues of saints on the small altar in the corner of the room.

"Your memories can't be right," Tianna said

through bitter tears. "I get sick. I bleed. I have pimples and scars from chicken pox. I had a broken collarbone! I can't be something the Atrox created, especially not something of irresistible beauty."

She stood, tromped to the refrigerator, and studied her blurred reflection in the chrome. "Look at me! My eyes are red and swollen, my lips are chapped and peeling, my face is cut, and my hair is stringy."

But even as she listed her complaints, she also saw how inexplicably beautiful she was, unnaturally so. She sobbed and clutched the edge of the counter to keep from falling.

When her strength returned, she grabbed her boots, sat down, tugged them on, and then stomped angrily toward the door. "You're wrong," she said, enraged. "I'll prove you are."

"*Es verdad.* You always knew you weren't like other kids." Jimena followed after her into the living room and touched her gently on the back. "Think of your dog."

Tianna bristled as the memory returned. She

and Jamie had been playing with a Frisbee. It had whirled into the street and their dog had chased it into a speeding car. Jamie had run back into the house screaming, but Tianna had picked up the mess of blood and bone and buried it in the backyard. She had willed herself to feel the grief her sister felt, but it had been a long time before she could experience such profound sorrow.

She sniffled, sensing Jimena had been in her mind viewing the memory with her. "My mother told me I'd probably become a surgeon and work in a trauma center. She said the world needed people like me, who didn't faint at the sight of blood. She said—" Tianna stopped suddenly, remembering the meticulous way her mother had reinterpreted every event in her life to give her confidence and make her feel normal.

"She let you see a good side to everything you did or said," Jimena continued for her. "Even when you felt—"

"Even when I felt I wasn't good." Tianna stared at the clock on top of the television. She had less than an hour left. "But I was never brutal or cruel or evil," she added, hating the feel of the last word on her tongue. "I learned to love and feel compassion."

"Your mother fed you moon dew, a magic elixir, to give you heart and soul," Jimena explained.

Tianna remembered walking barefoot in the wet grass, sipping sweet liquid from honeysuckle blossoms under a full moon. She had thought it was only a game.

"My mother loved the moonlight," she said sadly. Tears spilled from her eyes again and she felt the warmth of her mother's devotion, love, and care, and then her head shot up as another idea jumped into her mind. "You're mistaken. I know you are. You must have me confused with someone else, because Maggie said I was—"

Jimena touched her lips and silenced her. "Maggie knew who you were and gave you the moon amulet, hoping the charm would protect you," Jimena explained. "Any of her deceptions came from love, and were attempts to safeguard you from your destiny."

Tianna felt as if someone had stolen her soul, and then with a shudder she realized she had never had one, but the face of her mother burst protectively into her mind, along with the delicately sweet memory of moon dew. She did have a soul. She knew she must. She looked up at Jimena. "What is my destiny? Is it the *becoming* everyone is talking about?"

"I don't know yet," Jimena replied. "I only know the Atrox plans to use you to bring unimaginable sorrows to earth."

"With my telekinesis," Tianna muttered, feeling terrible frustration. "Why else would I have such a strong power? I'm afraid I'll be unable to control it and I'll go on a rampage, destroying everything."

"I don't think it was a power at first," Jimena said. "It was only a way for you to go back and forth between Nefandus and earth. It's possible you taught yourself how to use the energy to move things."

"Maybe," Tianna answered. "But if the Atrox planned to use me all along, then why did it punish Justin and Mason and make them outcasts for killing my family?"

Jimena stared at her, and Tianna knew she didn't want to hear the answer. She grabbed the doorknob, sensing that the words, once spoken, would have the ability to harm her.

"Selene unknowingly made a horrible error when she stole you from the Atrox," Jimena said sadly. "The abduction was always part of its plan. It wanted you to grow up as human as possible."

"Human?" Tianna asked, feeling the room spin. "Are you saying I'm not even human?"

Jimena's silence gave her the answer she needed. Tianna turned the doorknob.

"Don't go," Jimena said and tried to stop her. "You're safer here with me. The rest of my memories will return soon, and then we'll know what to do."

"What if it takes too long?" Tianna opened the door. "What good is it for you to come down to earth if you can't remember why you came or what we need to do? You should have stayed in heaven."

"Do you think I want the Atrox to win?" Jimena grabbed her wrist. "There must be a way to defeat it. *Es lo que mas me preocupa.* It's the only thing on my mind. I'm trying."

"Something else is holding your memories back," Tianna said sadly. "Maybe the Atrox is stronger than you think."

"That may be true, but for now you shouldn't do what you're planning," Jimena said, as if she had read Tianna's thoughts. "It won't work."

Tianna stepped into the dark hallway and shook her head with cheerless determination. "I'll spend my life running. If the Atrox can't find me, then it can't use me to harm others. Maybe I can stop 'the becoming.'"

"That won't work as easily as you think," Jimena warned.

Tianna ignored her, turned, and walked away.

CHAPTER TWENTY-SEVEN

IT WAS ALMOST midnight, minutes before Tianna was to meet her destiny. The storm had subsided and the moon had claimed the sky, its radiance weaving a protective web around her. She had come to the deserted stretch of beach to pray to the Good in the universe. At first she had tried to bargain with her fate. Having done that, she felt a deep sadness creep over her. Jimena was right. She couldn't run. She realized that now. The

Atrox would destroy anyone she cared about until she surrendered to it. Shannon and Todd were safe, but for how long? And what would happen to Derek? She sensed intuitively that Vanessa, Catty, and Serena were still alive, the Atrox holding them hostage until she gave in. What would happen to them if she didn't turn herself over?

Frothing waves pounded the shore, their rhythm calming her. She had been fearful that she would use her telekinetic power to destroy, but her power had settled deep inside her.

She took off her boots, delaying the moment, and left them in the sand. She walked barefoot down the shoreline, the sea spume cold beneath her feet. She should have left L.A. when she had first gotten the urge to move on. She hadn't listened to her instincts because she had so desperately wanted a normal life. Now all was lost to her.

She climbed onto a jetty and faced the full luminescence of the moon. She willed it to strike her down and end her profane existence. A wave crashed against the boulders and sprayed over her, but nothing more happened. She licked the salt-water from her lips. Her time had come.

Immediately a shadow slithered around her, but she didn't fear it. She had been expecting an envoy from the Atrox. Stanton materialized beside her, his black cape billowing behind him. Emblazoned on his shoulder was a crest depicting two hands holding the eternal flame of evil, the symbol for the Prince of the Night. Sea mist gathered and made a delicate pattern on the silk.

"I'm ready." She held her breath and waited for him to take her to the Atrox. When nothing happened, she blinked and looked at him.

"I haven't come to take you to the Atrox," he whispered hoarsely. "I'm not a threat."

"Then why are you here?" she asked.

"The Atrox has Serena, Catty, and Vanessa." His grief was obvious.

"I know," she said. "And now it will have me."

He studied her carefully, but she had no sense that he was trying to hypnotize her. "You can weaken it so I can rescue them."

"What can I do?" she said, wondering if she

could trust Stanton. Instinct told her that she could. Besides, what did she have to lose?

He pulled back his cape and his fingers grasped the hilt of a sword. He drew it from the scabbard and pointed it at the sky. Moonlight reflected off the blade in dazzling rainbow lights. The sword seemed to be carved from gray stone.

"Maggie used this centuries back to bind the Atrox to its shadow. Do it again for Serena, Catty, and Vanessa." He offered it to her.

As Tianna grasped the pommel, energy vibrated up her arm. Maggie's love enveloped her, as if her spirit still lingered inside the cold stone. "But I thought using weapons only made the Atrox stronger."

"The sword was forged with love out of rock cut from the moon," he explained. "It will bind the Atrox to its shadow so it can no longer transform."

"How do I use it?" she asked, resolute.

"Find a way to make the Atrox take its human form," Stanton spoke quickly now, as if he sensed time slipping away. "Then plunge the sword down, through shoulder and bone, to where a heart would beat if the Atrox had one." His eyes narrowed, his need for revenge clear. "Do this for Serena, Vanessa, and Catty."

"I will." She slipped the sword down inside her pant leg. The blade felt smooth and comforting against her skin. "Won't the Atrox sense my treachery?"

"The Atrox can't feel love," Stanton explained. "Think only of the ones you care for and it will be blinded to your plan."

Tianna suddenly understood why the Atrox had never been able to see Stanton's devotion to Serena. She nodded and felt a surge of energy. "I'll do it."

"Thank you." Stanton gratefully cupped her face in his hands and let his knowledge slip inside her head. "Do you see what will happen to you when you do this?"

She nodded. "I understand."

"Do you?" he asked, even though she sensed that he was reading her thoughts. "Tell me."

"When I bind the Atrox, I'll bind myself as

well. Maggie was able to escape because she was created by the Good in the universe. I won't have that hope. The Atrox is my creator." The words made her wince, and she closed her mind; she couldn't bear to imagine spending eternity with such unthinkable evil. "It's my choice. I'll do this for everyone I've loved that it has destroyed."

"It's the only way to stop your *becoming*," he said, as if that would give her solace. Then he kissed her cheek and started to fall back, dissolving into a flicker of shade.

"Stanton," she asked, stopping him. "What is this *becoming* everyone has been talking about?"

His words drifted to her as the wind swept his shadow away. "*Becoming* the mother of the Atrox's child."

CHAPTER TWENTY-EIGHT

TIANNA TOOK A deep breath. She didn't know how to summon the Atrox, but just thinking about doing so made words gather on her tongue. A deeper instinct told her that the invocation, once spoken, would unleash hell. She concentrated, summoning all her strength, and then, determined, turned her back on the moon.

The sword lay flat against her leg inside her jeans. Its energy vibrated through her and gave her courage. She lifted her hands in supplication, and the starry sky looked down on her with cruel contempt.

"I call my master, the Atrox!" Her entreaty came out bold and powerful, echoing down the beach. Her heart lurched at the sound of her own voice, and sickening terror gripped her stomach. She closed her eyes and tried to reason that she had no other choice. The urge to run was over-whelming. Instead, she stood her ground and stretched her fingers, linking herself to the night.

"Lord of Darkness," she rasped. "Take me as your betrothed."

The air throbbed with an ancient primordial rhythm. Waves surged, crashing over the rocks, and seawater sprayed her back with an icy cold. She shivered, feeling abandoned, unwanted, and her arms fell down to her sides.

"Hello, Tianna," a soft voice said.

A chill rushed through her, rousing an instinctive dread. She glanced up.

Ethan stood at the top of the cliff above her, his black slacks flapping in the breeze. He walked slowly down to her, his steps easy on the steep rock face. When he reached her, he held out his hand, and his thoughts breathed across her mind. *I'll take you to the Atrox, but you must come of your own free will.*

"I come freely." She extended her arm, and something inside her collapsed. Hot tears slid down her cheek, and her trembling fingers skimmed over his outstretched palm. His skin felt surprisingly warm.

She stared into his strange eyes and kept her mind focused on all the ones she had loved and lost: her parents; her little sister, Jamie; Maggie; Derek; the other Daughters.

"Take me to the Atrox," she said, terrified her plan would be uncovered. If Ethan embraced her, he would feel the sword hilt pressed painfully against her ribs. Did it bulge beneath her sweatshirt? She felt his presence in her thoughts and quickly turned to a memory of her mother standing in the full moon's glow.

"I'll take you to Nefandus." Ethan smiled sardonically, clasped her hand, and glanced at her right leg.

She felt immeasurably foolish now, convinced he had caught her deceit, but then he looked out to sea and his body slowly faded, turning to a silken mist. His shadow rolled around her, grazing her face, and she began to turn to sooty gloom.

For one terrifying moment she feared the sword wouldn't change with her, but seconds later she sensed its soothing comfort.

They soared into the night, forming a nebulous shape flitting across the ivory face of the moon. Her heart already missed the purity of life. The soft roar of surf flooded through her, filling her with intense yearning, and she whispered a sweet good-bye to the long stretch of shore.

With a burst of speed, they rose steadily higher, and then, without warning, Ethan dropped her. The molecules of her body slammed back together, and she plummeted, her stomach rising. She stared at the rocky outcropping below and tried to scream, but the shrieking wind stole her voice. She knew in an instant that the Atrox had sensed her treachery after all and had condemned her to die.

She tried to summon her energy to stop the fall, but the wind slapped her power away. A storm of glowing embers and sparks swirled around her, but she couldn't make her telekinetic force seize her body and slow her descent.

She had gone up against the Atrox once before and lost. What had made her think she could win against it this time? She twisted around, her hair whipping into her eyes, and struggled to see the moon before she died.

Black lightning flashed in front of her, exploding across the sky. Red afterimages blinded her. A thunderclap boomed, rumbling and reverberating across the air. Then a huge, spectral cloud swept around her, eclipsing all light, and stopped her fall.

You belong to me, the Atrox said soothingly, cradling her in its evil miasma. Its malevolent spirit surged through her, tainting her blood and pulsing in her veins, leaving in her mouth the sweetly bitter taste of ancient tombs and mold.

Shadows writhed over her with sensual slowness, lulling her with each caress, and the faint scent of sulfur permeated the air. Something familiar stirred inside her, awakening, and she no longer felt afraid. She stretched, enjoying the sensation of soft air wrapping around her. She slid her hands down her body, reveling in a primitive feeling of wickedness. Her fingers caught on the sword's hilt. She jerked her hand away and jarred the blade, making the tip slice her ankle. Pain shot up her leg.

Do you have something you want to do? The Atrox asked.

The words slipped across her mind.

"Yes," she whispered.

Her will to fight had vanished, replaced with only one desire: to please her master. She drew the sword from her waistband. The blade licked her thigh and its energy flared in warning, igniting her blood on the point. She let it fall. It hit something solid, as if she were still standing on the rocky shore. The clatter rang into the universe and echoed through her with terrible, foreboding force.

For the briefest moment she hesitated, unsure, but then the swarming dark twirled lazily around her. She closed her eyes again and fell back, dissolving in the Atrox's embrace. She was *becoming*.

CHAPTER TWENTY-NINE

"B E HUMAN FOR ME, so I can love you as I would my husband," Tianna pleaded.

Abruptly the shadow cloud raced away and she realized she had always been standing in a huge bedroom. She swung around, looking for the Atrox, her heart beating crazily. A savage fire crackled in the hearth, but the blaze did little to warm the air. Her breath made a white vapor.

Candles lined the mantel, flames stretching

up the wicks and releasing a sweet, captivating scent, but she caught another stench underneath, something foul that lingered unpleasantly in her lungs.

She took a step. Blood dripped from the cut on her ankle and pattered to the gray stone floor. Long black tapers shed more light from gold candelabra on either side of a bed canopied with dark draperies. The silky comforter was thrown back, revealing glossy sheets.

Footsteps sounded and she took a deep breath, anxiously waiting, but half fearing that a grizzled old man with sparse hair and bulging facial veins would walk from the shroud of dark forming in the far corner of the room. She stepped closer.

Three wolves slipped from the interweaving shadows and padded slowly to the fire. They whimpered, yellow eyes gazing at her, then curled together on the hearthstone. The darkness spun into the silhouette of a man, and Ethan stepped out, black threads of vapor rippling behind him.

"Ethan," she whispered and smiled, craving

his touch. She couldn't quite remember why she had been so reluctant and fearful to be with him before.

He walked toward her, teasing her with his slow pace, as if he understood how much she desired him now. At last he stood next to Tianna and wrapped his arms around her.

His touch made her shudder. Her future was now bound to his. She closed her eyes and let him enter her mind. The luscious, trancelike feeling of melding with him was greater than any normal embrace, but then he started to kiss her cheek, and his cold lips stung her skin.

"You created me?" Tianna asked, shivering, her breath quickening.

"I did," he whispered, cupping her face possessively between his hands. His eyes pierced hers, dangerous and unyielding.

Revulsion shivered through her but she was desperate to know more. "Like a clone?"

"No," he answered and his hands, once warm, now frosty, slipped down her neck and over her shoulders to her hands.

She ached from wanting him, and his tenderness almost made her believe he had the capacity to love, but his flesh, more dead than alive now, leeched life from her. Energy seeped from her fingers, and her heartbeat slowed.

"Then, did you use magic?" She stopped and frowned.

"Magic? Yes, that's closer." Shadows coiled around his pallid face. She wasn't sure if the dark mists emanated from him or if they were separate, swirling about the room.

"But I must have come from something. What was it?" she asked.

"I copied the miracle of creation," he said. "If you hadn't become so tainted by the moon you'd remember when I breathed life into you."

"Tell me," she whispered and parted her lips, waiting for his kiss.

"You were born from the first stirrings of the dark as the sun gave way to night. The Fates helped me. No one could stop me once they had agreed. Even Zeus had to bow to their decree. They gathered the power of the moon, and

Klotho spun the thread of life and gave it to me. Then Lachesis wove a cloth that reached to infinity to give you immortality. Atropos gave me her cruel scissors so you'd never face death."

"But the failures—" Tianna started to say, thinking of Mary.

"There were too many." He nodded. "Treading on the boundary between death and birth is delicate, and countless mistakes were made."

"But if you could create me, then why not create a son?" she asked.

The suggestion seemed to anger him. "My son will have a mother to nurture him. No human has ever measured up. I tested many, but all failed me. Now I have you."

"Am I good enough or evil enough to be its mother?" she asked.

He ignored her question and kissed her. Frost covered her lips, spreading out to her cheeks. He pulled back.

"Maybe I shouldn't have given you so much intelligence," he said, as if she had asked too many questions, "and only given you the need to destroy—but then you would never have come to love me."

"Love?" she repeated. The word hung oddly in the air and she couldn't quit recall what it meant. But then its sound filled her with an odd glow and she remembered Jamie, her mother and father, the Daughters, Derek, and Maggie. Memories of them broke the spell seducing her. Desire slipped away and was replaced by fear.

"Why would you want love when you can't feel love yourself?" she bravely asked.

Ethan stepped away from her, angered, as if he coveted most what he could never possess.

She suddenly remembered the sword and the reason she had summoned the Atrox. She conjured a picture of the moon and hid her thoughts, then scanned the stone floor. She remembered dropping the sword, but where? She assumed that even when she had seemed to be lost in shadows, she had actually been in this room.

Then she saw her trail of blood, drops leading from where she stood now back to the bed. The hilt of the sword lay there, partially hidden among the folds of the canopy, uncannily luminous. Her heart sank. It was an impossible distance away.

"Tianna?" Ethan touched her shoulder, startling her. "You seem lost in reverie. What are you thinking?"

She didn't answer, because she could feel him in her mind, stronger than before, rushing through her thoughts. She attempted to hide her plan in a veil of love and took a step back. "When Selene gave me heart and soul—"

"Selene?" His eyes turned fierce, and he stretched out his hand, pointing at her.

Something inside her slipped. Panicked, she touched her chest, her fingers searching for the comforting pulse of her blood. She felt nothing.

He smiled at her, amused.

Her heart had stopped beating, and yet she breathed. Had he done that to her? Would he take her soul next?

"When Selene gave me heart and soul," she started again, stalling for time as she tried to think of a way to move over to the bed without raising his suspicions, "I became human, filled with dreams and desires. I always imagined that on my wedding night I would wear a beautiful white gown."

"Such foolishness." He sneered, but something in his expression told her he was pleased with her silliness. "Maybe I shouldn't have let Selene steal you from me."

A vapor twisted around his hand, weaving and tightening until it glistened and turned to black satin. Then a nightgown appeared, clutched in his fist. He handed it to her.

"Thank you," she whispered, and she strolled to the bed, her eyes intent on the radiant blade. She stopped when her toes were inches from the sword. She felt suddenly shy and embarrassed, but if her plan were to work, she had no choice.

With her back to Ethan, she peeled off her sweatshirt and blouse. She could feel his gaze on her back, and a blush spread over her face, neck, and arms. She slipped the gown over her head, then reached up under the smooth material and pulled down her jeans. Craftily, she bent over, as if to free her foot, and she grabbed the hilt of the sword. She clutched it tightly, and power surged through her.

"Tianna!" Ethan called.

She froze. Had she been so easily caught? Slowly and carefully, she stood, then turned, keeping the sword stealthily hidden behind her. She held her head higher, her back straighter, imagining the moon. "What?" she asked.

"You're too shy." He smiled mockingly. "I thought I had created a temptress."

"In time, my creator," she said with a beguiling whisper. "Grant me one wish."

"What do you desire now?" He held one hand up, ready to conjure another luxury.

"Free the Daughters so I may destroy them myself." She tilted her head in a flirtatious way, and thought of her love for Derek. "You said I was created to destroy. Give me this gift so I can use my powers against them."

Ethan shot into her head, probing her mind, the cold tendrils of his thought searching for deceit.

Had she made a mistake in asking for that one favor? To keep her duplicity from him, she pictured her baby sister, Jamie, and the good times they had had playing together.

At last his mental hold slackened. "You are my perfect mate," he said. "Now you'll have your gift and my permission to destroy them. I'll give you Derek, also."

He shot his hand into the air, and shadows billowed from his fingers, rustling together to form a flat surface; then, projected over the mists, as if on a television screen, Serena, Catty, and Vanessa appeared, freed and running through the streets of Nefandus, their moon amulets sparkling brightly. The scene faded, and Derek's image emerged. He was still on the couch in the family room. He shook his head, as if awakening from a nightmare.

Her chest expanded with love, and tears filled her eyes. She blinked, so that her joy wouldn't give her away, and gripped the sword tightly behind her, her fingers numb and frozen onto the hilt. Then, with an audacious grin, she murmured,

"Come here, Ethan. I'm waiting for another kiss."

He smiled and stepped toward her, then closed his eyes and started to embrace her.

She swung the sword high over her head and plunged the blade into his shoulder, down into his chest.

His eyes flashed open.

"You created me to destroy," she said. "Now I have fulfilled my destiny."

CHAPTER THIRTY

BUT ETHAN DIDN'T dissolve. Fierce flames exploded around him in an unholy halo; his eyes widened, and he thrashed against the binding blade. The sword shimmered with white brilliance and cast a glorious glow about the room, its light outshining that of the fire and candle flames.

Tianna yanked on the pommel to pull the sword out and try again, but it had fused inside him and was melding into his flesh. She let go and stepped back, knowing she had succeeded.

"But at what price?" Ethan asked, reading her

mind. Shadow ropes whipped from him and lashed around her neck in a stranglehold. "No matter what you do you'll always be bound to me, existing in my evil eternity."

Ethan screamed and withered into a corpse. He struggled against the transformation back to phantom vapor. His humanlike existence ended, and the terrible energy of the Atrox spewed around Tianna, its breath filled with hatred and a need for revenge. It cut into her chest with razor-sharp ease and she felt her soul slipping from her.

"O Mater Luna, Regina nocis, adiuvo me nunc." She repeated the prayer Maggie had taught her to use in times of grave danger. The power of the words shimmered into the air, and suddenly she realized that she had always had two destinies: one stemming from her foul creation and another that she had created with the loving help of her mother and Selene. Every small choice she had made each day had woven another future, one against the decree of the Fates.

Suddenly, Catty, Serena, and Vanessa broke into the room and ran toward her. Tianna sensed intuitively that they had come to rescue her, in spite of the danger to themselves. The three Daughters joined hands, forming a ring around Tianna, and together they repeated the prayer Maggie had taught them. Then, silver moonlight appeared, cascading through the tall, narrow windows, even though Tianna knew it was impossible. No moon glowed in Nefandus. The cleansing luminescence cradled her and filled her with unbearable love and happiness. She stretched her arms toward the light, longing for its touch, and anxious to fall back into eternity.

Catty, Vanessa, and Serena each whispered their good-byes, and then everything became blindingly bright, each tiny sound magnified a thousandfold. This time something pure and longed-for penetrated her chest, and she joyously released her soul. Her spirit retreated from her body and rode on tranquil moonbeams, flowing upward, the strength of the universe pulling her away.

At last, Selene reached down and took her home.

Coming soon: the bad-boy companion
series to

DAUGHTERS OF THE MOON

SONS
OF THE
DARK

barbarian

"**O**BIE," A DEEP VOICE called.

Startled, Obie turned.

Two guys in faded black concert T-shirts
crouched nearby beneath a dry, dusty oleander
bush.

"The *Barbie*-girl is looking for you." The
skinny one pointed, and his studded leather cuff
slipped down his bone-thin arm.

Obie frowned and turned again.

Kirsten Ashton stood near the row of discarded desks. She smiled and raised her hand in a silly wave. Her shining curls and glossy, pink lips clashed with the stark black eyeliner, straight hair, and major attitude of the girls hanging out in Smokers' Alley.

She clutched her notebook against her chest and moved softly through the weeds, waving hi to everyone she passed, oblivious to their cold, silent stares. She had the regal confidence of all popular kids and assumed she'd be accepted anywhere.

Kirsten stopped in front of Obie. "I called your name three times. Didn't you hear me?" she asked sweetly, and cocked her head.

"No." Obie wondered what she wanted with him. She sat behind him in history class and usually acted as if he weren't even there. Not that he cared.

"I love your new song, 'Time Trap,'" she said with a flirty smile. "I heard it on the radio this morning. It's going to be a big hit."

"Thanks," he replied, only half listening to her. The feeling of alarm that had enveloped him earlier was fading, but he was still on edge, distracted by even the slightest movement around him.

"Your music makes me feel so much longing." She brushed a hand through her platinum-blond hair. Her silver nail polish matched the lines painted around her eyes. "Where do you get your inspiration?"

He shrugged, and, before Kirsten could say more, the warning bell rang, signaling the end of the lunch period. Kids stamped out their cigarettes and started back to class. Kirsten joined them.

But Obie didn't want to push in to the crush of kids sneaking back on to campus before the final bell. He charged off in the other direction and lunged between two overgrown Arizona cypresses. The scratchy branches snapped and cracked as he emerged from the other side, then sprinted across the basketball courts toward the front of the school.

Obie turned in to a breezeway and dodged around the kids hurrying to class. His boots pounded the concrete with a thumping noise louder than that of the rowdy yells and laughter.

He took the next corner too quickly and slammed into Allison Taylor. She had been standing with her friends, and now they broke apart, startled by his sudden appearance.

"Sorry." He caught Allison around the waist before she fell. Her dark hair swept over his chest, and her flowery perfume spun around him. He breathed in her fragrance like a thief and let his hands linger on her soft, warm skin. She reminded him of someone he had known before. "I didn't mean to knock you over," he said, apologizing.

Allison stepped back and looked down. "It's only a foot. I'll get a new one."

Her friends laughed.

She wore leather sandals, silver toe rings, and beaded strings of hemp around her thin ankles. A bruise was causing a swelling on the top of her foot. He felt like whisking her into his arms and carrying her to one of the picnic benches in the quad to make sure she was okay, but he controlled the impulse; such things weren't done here.

Allison turned back to her friends as if Obie weren't even standing there.

"I just got a chill," Allison said and rubbed the gooseflesh on her tanned arms. "Someone must have walked over my grave."

"That didn't give you the chill," Obie said, intruding again.

Allison's friends stared at him. Arielle adjusted her halter, as if Obie's presence made her uncomfortable, and Caitlin tugged nervously at her earring, waiting to see what Allison would do.

"Are you telling me it was the thrill of seeing you?" Allison asked, breaking the tension.

Arielle laughed too loudly, and Caitlin continued to stare.

"As if." Allison rolled her eyes and turned away from him again.

Obie continued slowly down the outside corridor to the other side of the classroom door, kids shoving around him, and settled back against the wall, alone. He turned back to watch Allison. She was the most popular girl at Turney High, and kids gathered around her as if she were a movie star handing out autographs. What would she have done if he had told her the true reason for her gooseflesh? He smirked, imagining her reaction, but in the end she wouldn't have believed him, and it would only have given her one more reason to make fun of him.

"She'll never go out with you," a sulky voice whispered. Kirsten stood beside him, spreading pink gloss on her lips. He hadn't heard her sidle up next to him.

"Like I care," he answered.

"Don't lie to me." Kirsten seemed annoyed. "Your crush is so obvious."

"Crush?"

"Anyone can see you're crazy in like with her."

"You're wrong," he said, finally understanding her choice of words. "I don't like her." No girl was worth the risk. He couldn't change what fate had made him.

LYNNE EWING is a screenwriter who also counsels troubled teens. In addition to writing all of the Daughters of the Moon books, she is the author of the new companion series Sons of the Dark. Ms. Ewing lives in Los Angeles, California.